"Take you

Holt's mouth ~~slowly slip t~~ just as slowly, she pushed her leggings down one leg and then the other, until she stepped free from them. Holt said nothing as he stared at her. He'd pictured her like this in his mind, with the firelight flickering softly over her. Her skin was paler, even creamier than the thin scrap of silk and lace she still wore. Her waist was so narrow, her legs slender as a wish and longer than he'd dreamed.

"Come here," he rasped.

"I will," Carly promised as she raised her hands to frame his face. "But I want you to know that this has nothing to do with my family or the business. I choose to do this because I want you. Only you."

He felt a streak of power, sharp and clean. The words were far more seducing than her scent, or even the pleasure her hands promised as she ran them down his chest to slip beneath his sweater. Suddenly unable to wait, he drew her down on the rug.

"I've wanted you from the first moment I saw you," he said. Then, taking her in his arms, he rolled her under him and covered her body with his....

Dear Reader,

I love New York City, and I've always wanted to set one of my stories there. So when my editor asked me to write a MANHUNTING book, I thought "Perfect!" What better place could there be to hunt down a man than in the corporate jungle of Manhattan?

My hero is CEO Holt Cassidy, cool and aloof, a true loner. Marriage is *not* on his agenda unless it figures in the bottom line. Then he meets Carly Carpenter, a bright, determined young woman whose one goal in life is to convince Holt that love *is* the bottom line!

I think Manhattan is a great place to fall in love, and the perfect place for these two characters to lead each other on a merry chase! I hope you enjoy the ride as much as I did.

All my best,

Carolyn Andrews

P.S. I love to hear from my readers. You can write to me at Harlequin Enterprises, 225 Duncan Mill Road, Don Mills, Ontario, Canada, M3B 3K9

Carolyn Andrews

Manhunting
in Manhattan

Sharon,
I hope you
enjoy Carly's story!

Carolyn Andrews

Harlequin Books

TORONTO • NEW YORK • LONDON
AMSTERDAM • PARIS • SYDNEY • HAMBURG
STOCKHOLM • ATHENS • TOKYO • MILAN
MADRID • WARSAW • BUDAPEST • AUCKLAND

To Aunt Rachel—
one of my biggest fans since the day I was born.
Thanks for everything. This one's for you.

ISBN 0-373-25773-2

MANHUNTING IN MANHATTAN

Copyright © 1998 by Carolyn Hanlon.

Printed in U.S.A.

1

SHE'D NEVER PROPOSED to a man before. That was reason enough to have cold feet. The last thing she needed was to step ankle-deep into a puddle of icy slush as she got out of the taxi. Her soaked calfskin boots squished as she hopped quickly onto the curb. Not a good sign.

She frowned down at her wet feet. Carly Carpenter believed in signs. But not enough to let them rule her life. Squaring her shoulders, she tightened her grip on her backpack and strode around the corner to the front entrance of Holt Cassidy's Manhattan apartment building. She was going to ignore her rather inauspicious arrival and concentrate on what she'd come to do.

"Convince Holt Cassidy to marry me." She spoke the words aloud. If she repeated the statement often enough, it might become more real. And perhaps it would even happen. Two feet from the door, she felt the confidence she'd shored up so carefully during a long and sleepless night begin to slip away.

Did she really intend to go up to a man's apartment at seven o'clock in the morning and propose marriage?

Was she crazy?

It was a question that had crossed her mind more than once. Ever since she'd arrived at the shocking realization that she wanted to get married. Of course, as a cultural anthropologist, she was quite familiar with the universal urge of the human being to mate. She'd simply believed that she was immune to it.

It wasn't that she had anything against marriage in general. She'd just decided a long time ago to keep her knowledge of it strictly academic. She'd lost her mother when she was only fifteen. And she'd experienced firsthand what it was like to step into her mother's shoes, raising her ten-year-old sister and supporting her father's career. When other girls her age were dreaming of Prince Charming, she'd been dreaming of independence. And after postponing college for four long years, she'd thought she'd found everything she'd ever wanted in the academic life.

Until lately.

Turning, Carly began to pace back and forth along the sidewalk. Lately, she'd been feeling...restless. At first, she'd blamed it on the fact that, after two years of doing field research on the island of Manilai, she was bored. But when her sister Jenna's letter had arrived, asking her to be the maid of honor at her wedding, Carly's feeling had suddenly crystallized into something quite different. Jealousy. And that shocked her.

At the corner, she whirled and continued to pace. What in the world was wrong with her? She'd just turned thirty. Was her biological clock sounding its alarm? Or perhaps living on an small South Seas island and studying the marriage customs of an isolated tribe had finally gotten to her. Maybe the primitive urge to mate was contagious.

When she once more reached the front door of the apartment building, Carly took a good look at her reflection, then shook her head. Shakespeare had always blamed the whole thing on moon madness. It was as good an explanation as any for why she was about to propose marriage to her younger sister's fiancé.

When Jenna had called her to her bedroom after midnight and revealed her plan to jilt Holt Cassidy and elope with her one true love, Carly had hoped she was just having a nightmare. But she wasn't. And although Jenna had sworn her to secrecy and refused to reveal the name of her lover or where they were eloping to, she'd been all too willing to describe the starring role she expected Carly to play in the unfolding drama.

Carly could still picture her sister sitting there on the foot of her bed, radiating happiness and telling her that instead of being a maid of honor next Friday, she would just have to be Holt Cassidy's substitute bride!

And Jenna had said it so calmly, as if she were Miss America simply turning over her crown to the first runner-up. Worst of all, Carly had agreed to the plan!

Obviously, she'd been in shock. She still was. That's why her feet were so cold and her hands were numb. She stamped her boots, and after shifting the strap of her backpack to her other shoulder, she curled her fingers into fists and drew them up into the sleeves of her jacket.

At the present moment, Carly was in total empathy with her younger sister. More than anything, she wanted to run away, too. But not to go on a honeymoon. No, she'd be content to hail a cab, go back home and hide under the covers until someone woke her up from this horrible dream. But that wasn't going to happen.

Suffering from shock or not, she was going to take her sister's place. Facing her reflection in the glass door, she reached slowly for the handle. Desperate times called for desperate measures. But before she stormed into the lion's den, it might be wise to review her strategy.

Dropping her hand to her side, she turned and crossed the street, then walked quickly to the corner, where she could catch a glimpse of the Hudson River. Living on an island for a year, she'd learned that looking out over the water helped her to think more clearly. Holt would have a good view of the Hudson from his apartment on the fifteenth floor. But today the mist was so thick it clung to the river like a shroud. For just a second as she stood there staring at the dense gray swirls rising from the water, Carly had the distinct feeling that she was looking into her future.

Ridiculous. She was going to do this. After all, it was the logical solution to everyone's problems—her family's as well as Holt's. As frustrating as her family could be, Carly couldn't prevent a smile from curving her lips at the thought of her father, the flamboyant Calvin Carpenter, who'd turned a small herbal tea company into Carpenter Enterprises, a successful health food conglomerate. And even Jenna had her redeeming qualities, when she wasn't plunging them all into a crisis!

Carly shoved her hands into her pockets and began to pace once more. If only their mother hadn't died, things might have been different. Her father might not have fought against his overwhelming grief by burying himself entirely in the business. With less stress, Calvin Carpenter might not have had to undergo triple bypass surgery six months ago. And then Jenna might not have had to agree to a marriage of convenience to ensure the future of Carpenter Enterprises.

When she reached the spot directly across from Holt's building, Carly whirled and paced back to the corner again. Thinking about what might have been wasn't going to solve her present problem. The fact was that on his doctors' advice, her father had to pass over the management of the company to someone. And that someone was Holt Cassidy.

According to Jenna, Holt's background was something of a mystery. Calvin had let it slip once that Holt had been orphaned at the age of four and had spent the rest of his childhood in a series of foster homes. Other than that, all Jenna had been able to tell her about Holt was that he'd come to her father for a loan a year ago, and Calvin, impressed with his business plan, had hired him on the spot to prevent Holt from becoming a formidable competitor.

Carly didn't doubt for a minute that Holt would make a *very* formidable competitor. Her first thought when she'd met him at dinner the night before was that he'd handle himself just as well in an alley as he would in a boardroom. Even now she could picture the new CEO of Carpenter Enterprises clearly. He'd made quite an impression on her. And she was still trying to analyze why.

There was that moment when they'd been introduced and he'd taken her hand. She'd felt something then, like a little jolt of electricity. Or recognition? Whatever it was, it had made her very aware of him for the rest of the evening.

But then, she couldn't imagine anyone being in the same room with Holt Cassidy and not being aware of him. And it wasn't just his looks, though the lean, raw-boned face and the thick dark hair curling over his ears and collar were certainly striking. It wasn't merely his size, either. Though he had a good ten inches on her, he wasn't quite six feet tall. And then there were those eyes. She hadn't had time to notice their color when she'd been introduced, but she'd felt them on her more than once at dinner. And even from a distance, they'd been...disturbing. Oh, yes, there was definitely something about Holt Cassidy.

Jenna had described him as a cool, corporate shark. But what her sister had viewed as coolness, Carly saw as the simple patience of a predator. And she suspected that what lurked beneath the surface was anything but cool. As an anthropologist, she'd studied a lot of cultures, and she'd recognized Holt Cassidy's type immediately. Centuries ago, he'd have been a ruler. Not some soft aristocrat who'd inherited his throne, but a warrior who'd snatched it away from a weaker opponent.

As a shiver raced down her spine, Carly pulled her jacket tighter and turned to look at Holt's apartment building again. In the primitive tribe she'd been studying for the past two years, he'd have led the hunters. Only the most beautiful young women would have had the courage to set their sights on him.

With a shake of her head, Carly pushed the thought out of her mind. She needed to boost her confidence, not destroy it. Turning, she began to pace again. From a logical standpoint, Holt had every reason to accept her as a substitute bride. Jenna had described the details quite clearly. To make sure that control of Carpenter Enterprises stayed in the family, Calvin had arranged a private merger of sorts between Holt, his handpicked successor, and his daughter Jenna. Everything had been signed, sealed and delivered. On Friday, when Holt Cassidy married into the family, he would become the new CEO and gain control of fifty-one percent of the family-owned stock.

The marriage would benefit the company, too. When Calvin had undergone surgery, Carpenter Enterprises' stock had taken a dip on the stock market. But at the announcement of the Cassidy-Carpenter wedding plans, the company's stock had regained its earlier losses and jumped ahead five points. So there was every reason for Holt to go through with the wedding even if there was a last-minute switch in brides.

So what was she waiting for? She wanted to get married, and her sister had dropped a ready-made groom into her lap. All she had to do was... "Convince Holt Cassidy to marry me. Convince Holt Cassidy to marry me." She began reciting the litany in her head again. And if she failed...?

Carly realized that it wasn't just her feet turning to ice anymore. It was her whole body. The numbness was spreading quickly from her wet feet to her knees and on up to her stomach. She felt paralyzed! If she didn't move soon, she was going to freeze to death.

Focusing all her energy on her feet, Carly placed one carefully in front of the other until she made it across the street. With each step the numbness faded. Climbing up on the curb, she strode toward the glass door of the apartment building.

She wasn't going to fail. Logically, Holt Cassidy just couldn't say no. Everything that she'd learned about him had convinced her that he was a reasonable man with one goal in life. He wanted to guide Carpenter Enterprises into the twenty-first century. If he married her on Friday, he could still do that. And surely she could talk a reasonable man into allowing her to maintain her independence. They could each have their cake and eat it, too, Carly assured herself as she reached for the door. Her hand was only inches away from the handle when a sharp jerk on the strap of her backpack spun her around.

She found herself staring at a boy no older than sixteen or seventeen. But his eyes were hard and desperate. She understood the desperation. She was feeling it herself when she gave her backpack a good yank. The boy held on.

"I've got money in my pocket. Let go of my bag and I'll give it to you," she offered as they began a tug-of-war with her backpack.

The boy said nothing. Carly thought of screaming, but the street had been deserted since she'd stepped from the cab.

"Look, there's no money in the bag. Let me keep it, and you can have everything in my pocket. Maybe fifty dollars. I won't even call the police." She tried to dig in her heels, but her boots were so wet that they began to slide along the sidewalk. The moment she felt some traction, she gave the bag another sharp tug. This time the boy lost ground, but she heard the strap start to rip. He was shouting names at her. She had to raise her voice to be heard. "Let go and you can have my wallet. You won't have to fence cash!"

This time when the boy tugged, she shot forward, nearly losing her balance. Then there was a shout that had him turning and racing away like a rocket. Carly pitched backward, landing smack in a pile of slush.

But she still had her backpack. Hugging it to her, she sat for a minute to catch her breath as the icy water seeped into her clothes. Even from the rear, she'd recognized the man who'd raced past her after the boy. Holt Cassidy wearing a sleek black running outfit. Without the corporate suit and tie, he looked different, more dangerous. Much more like a warrior. The instant he reappeared at the corner, she scrambled to her knees.

"Carly? What are you doing here?" he asked as his fingers closed around hers.

His hand wasn't smooth. Perhaps it was the slight abrasiveness of his palm rubbing against hers that sent the tingle radiating up her arm like an electric shock. Or perhaps she'd just accidentally stepped on a live wire with her wet boots. Either way, she lost her balance for just a second, and as she leaned against him, she had a quick, clear impression of steel, hard and unyielding. And heat. It pulled at her. Startled, she gazed up at him. His eyes. She hadn't noticed their color before. Gray like the mists that swirled thick and mysterious above the river. Her future?

HOLT PULLED CARLY to her feet, but he didn't immediately release his grip on her hand. It was a way of testing himself. Last night when they'd been introduced for the first time, they'd stood just as they were doing now, palm pressed against palm. For only a moment. But he'd felt something. It had bothered him all during dinner. And he'd awakened this morning worrying about it.

Though he hadn't met Carly before, he'd heard about her. Calvin's intellectual daughter. The older man was always bragging about how smart she was, the degrees she'd earned. His office was littered with pictures. But there'd been nothing in the photos to prepare Holt for the unexpected and elemental pull he'd felt when he'd held her hand.

At first he'd tried to convince himself it was merely simple attraction for a pretty woman. He'd put that theory to the test during dinner. But Carly wasn't nearly as pretty as her sister Jenna. Studying her features one by one, he couldn't find anything that would cause his eyes to return to her over and over. She wore her blond hair in a short, boyish cut. Her nose was too short, and the honey gold tan didn't quite cover the sprinkle of freckles. He'd gotten the impression she was almost too slender beneath the drab, boxy jacket and slacks she'd worn.

Perhaps it was all the energy and enthusiasm he'd felt when she'd talked about her work. And then she'd suddenly smiled at him as she was doing right now, and he realized that he'd been dead wrong about her not being pretty.

"What are you doing here, Carly?" Holt asked.

"Fighting for my life, it would seem."

Holt frowned. "Didn't anyone ever tell you not to argue with a mugger?"

"I wasn't arguing. Merely negotiating. I made him a cash offer if he would leave my backpack. It has my secret supply of coffee in it."

"Coffee?" Holt asked.

"Shocking, isn't it? One of Calvin Carpenter's daughters, raised from the cradle on herbal teas, is a coffee addict. I'm depending on you to keep my little secret. Especially from Dad. He'll think I've betrayed—"

"Do you mean to tell me that you fought with that street thug over coffee?" Holt asked in astonishment. "This is New York City, not some isolated South Seas island where people probably still live by the golden rule. Next time, don't negotiate. You could have gotten yourself killed."

Carly lifted her chin. "Well, then thank you for saving my life. But I don't like it when someone tries to take what's mine. And if the rule of the day is to give in to muggers, it's no wonder they feel so at home here in the Big Apple." Suddenly she shivered. "Besides, I'm more likely to die of pneumonia if I don't change out of these clothes. How about saving my life again by inviting me in?"

"C'mon." Shrugging out of his jacket, Holt wrapped it around her, then hurried her through the doors of his building.

FIFTEEN MINUTES LATER, Carly stepped out of a hot shower and toweled her hair. Once inside the apartment, Holt had hustled her silently into the bathroom and provided her with a pair of gray sweats. After rolling up the sleeves and legs and pulling them on, she turned warily to the full-length mirror on the bathroom door. From what she could make out through the steam, the whole outfit looked like something one of Snow White's dwarves would have tossed into a reject pile. But at least she was warm.

And her short reprieve was just about over. Grimly, Carly hitched up her pants, opened the door and walked down the narrow hallway. In the archway to the living room, she paused. And then as her mouth went dry, she stared. Holt was standing at the window with his back to her, watching snow swirl down.

The black T-shirt and running pants fit him like a second skin, blatantly revealing the smoothly honed muscles in his shoulders and his arms. And his legs. She couldn't take her eyes off him. Suddenly, she wanted to touch him. She couldn't remember an urge this strong before. More than anything, she wanted to run her hands over his shoulders and the bare skin of his arms.

Carly curled her fingers into fists. As a little girl, she'd often been tempted to touch her mother's iron when it was heating up. She could still remember being burned. But that had never prevented her from being tempted to touch it again.

Drawing in a deep, steadying breath, she deliberately shifted her gaze away from Holt to examine the rest of his lair. The apartment was small. A tiny galley of a kitchen was tucked in by a counter and stools at one end of the room. At the other, a fireplace boasted a pair of serious-looking swords above its mantel and a fur rug on its hearth. The rest of the furnishings were sparse, just a desk and the two chairs that faced each other across it.

Oddly enough, Carly found the room inviting. Maybe because the copper-bottomed pots that hung above the stove looked well used and well cared for. Or perhaps it was because the desk gleamed with a satiny sheen and smelled faintly of lemon oil. And then there was the silver tray nearby, which held an electric teakettle, a selection of Carpenter teas and two handpainted china mugs. Obviously, Holt Cassidy was a man who chose carefully the things he surrounded himself with, and then he took care of them. It was becoming clear to Carly why Calvin trusted him to run Carpenter Enterprises.

She shifted her gaze back to Holt. Somehow it had been easier to plan a proposal when he'd been more of a stereotype, the cool, corporate shark Jenna had described. She couldn't allow that image to blur and start thinking of him as a person. A man who'd just been abandoned by his fiancée. Carly was suddenly struck by how alone he looked standing in front of the window.

When he turned to look at her, his eyes clashed with hers. The image in Carly's mind shifted again. Here was the man she'd met at dinner last night. She could handle him.

"What can I do for you?" he asked, striding toward her.

"I could really use a cup of coffee."

"I heated some water." He lifted the kettle from the desk. "But all I can offer you is tea."

She smiled at him. "Just a cup of hot water will do." Fetching her backpack from the small foyer where she'd left it earlier, she joined him at the desk. "I brought my own coffee, remember?"

The memory of watching Carly being dragged slowly but surely along the street by a young thug was still fresh in Holt's mind. Women seldom surprised him. But Carly Carpenter had already managed to do that more than once. Filling two mugs with water, he handed her one, then added a tea bag to his own. He was about to ask her again what she wanted, when he suddenly became fascinated by what she was doing.

The world was full of tea-making rituals. He'd witnessed several firsthand in his travels in the merchant marine. But he couldn't ever recall anyone making a ritual out of fixing a cup of instant coffee. Yet that's just what Carly was doing. The preciseness of the way she measured the coffee granules, the care with which she added them to the mug and stirred indicated to Holt that this was something she'd practiced over and over. Then, closing her eyes, she inhaled the aroma trapped in the steam, and finally she took a sip. From the look on her face, it might have been the nectar of the gods she was drinking.

Though he preferred tea, Holt didn't really mind

coffee when it was well brewed. But instant coffee had always reminded him of diluted mud. Curious, he asked, "How did a Carpenter ever manage to become a coffee drinker?"

Carly grinned at him. "The forbidden-fruit syndrome. It's always irresistible, don't you think?" She took another drink. "I suppose there was some teenage rebellion involved, too. But the truth is, I really love the stuff."

"What about the caffeine?" Holt asked. "Carpenter Enterprises has several pamphlets—"

Carly stopped him with a raised hand. "I've read them all. Give me a pop quiz on those pamphlets, and I'll ace it." She paused to take another swallow of her coffee, enjoying it thoroughly. "I think that during college and grad school, I drank so much of this stuff that I've built up an immunity. It doesn't even keep me awake anymore." She set her mug down on the tray. "But I didn't come here to talk about my addiction to caffeine."

"I didn't think so," Holt said.

Carly clasped her hands tightly together. "The truth is, I've come to ask you to marry me instead of Jenna."

For a moment Holt said nothing. He didn't move, either. Carly thought of the sudden paralysis she'd felt when she'd been standing on the sidewalk outside. She'd almost turned into a statue just thinking about her proposal. Hearing it seemed to be having the same effect on Holt. Except for those eyes. They continued to study her, revealing nothing at the same time that they stared right into her very soul. Suddenly she had to move. She paced quickly to the wall, then turned back. He still hadn't moved. Squaring her shoulders, she said, "Before you jump at the chance, perhaps I'd better explain."

"It might be enlightening."

"Jenna...it seems that sometime during the past few months, my sister met someone. No, she more than *met* this person. She..." Pausing, Carly moved a little closer, then said the words in a rush. "She met him and fell in love with him, and last night she eloped with him. I'm sorry."

Holt still said nothing.

"You have a perfect right to be angry. I..." At a loss for words, Carly studied him for a minute. She would have given up her whole jar of instant coffee for one little clue as to what Holt was thinking. He looked so alone just standing there. Then she remembered her own first reaction to Jenna's story, and she started toward him. "You're shocked, of course. So was I. Jenna only told me her plans after you'd left last night. After everyone was in bed. And I agreed to take her place. I mean, there has to be a wedding, right? And Jenna said you probably wouldn't mind having a substitute bride."

Suddenly, Carly stopped. And it wasn't simply because she'd walked right to the edge of the desk. She stopped because she couldn't think of one more thing to say. What had seemed so logical last night now sounded absurd!

She threw her hands up. "I can't do this. I thought I could. I promised Jenna I would take care of everything. I'd just go to your apartment first thing this morning and convince you to marry me. Then—" she waved a hand "—on to my next appointment."

Whirling away, Carly paced to the wall and back again to the desk. "What was Jenna thinking of? First running around behind your back, then running off in the middle of the night! Deserting you! If she were here..." Carly met Holt's eyes squarely. "If she were here, I'd strangle her."

Her eyes narrowed. She could have sworn his lips had twitched. "You're laughing at me."

"No," Holt said. But she saw his lips twitch again.

"You *are* laughing at me. Well—" she fisted her hands on her hips "—I'm glad one of us is having fun. This is the first time in my life I've proposed to anyone, and I'm dressed like Clarabelle the clown!"

This time Holt laughed, and the strong, clear sound filled the room. "To tell you the truth, it's my first proposal, too."

"And it's hilarious, right?" She'd blown it, but for some reason the knot of nerves in her stomach started to melt.

"Well, strangling Jenna might be a little drastic," Holt pointed out. "You'd be arrested for murder, and I'd be left without even a substitute bride."

"True." Carly struggled against the laughter she felt bubbling up but failed. As it escaped, she felt the rest of her tension ease. And then she studied the man standing in front of her. She hadn't ever seen Holt Cassidy smile before. When he did, his eyes lightened, warmed. And if she stood there looking into them for one more minute, she was going to completely forget what she'd come here to accomplish. "Look, since this is a first proposal for both of us, why don't we think of it as a rehearsal? I'll go out, and when I come back in, I'll do better."

"That won't be necessary," Holt said, and his smile began to fade. He should have put an end to this right from the beginning. He couldn't have said why he didn't. Except that for a few moments there, he hadn't been able to take his eyes off Carly Carpenter. There was something about her...but this was hardly the time for idle curiosity. "You don't have to offer yourself in your sister's place."

"Yes, I do. Jenna explained everything. I took notes." Grabbing her backpack, Carly pulled out note cards and waved them at Holt. "See. This is another reason why I couldn't let that thug steal my bag. If I'd remembered them earlier, it would have been a much better proposal. I always do better with notes." Shuffling through them, she selected one. "For starters, Jenna said that Carpenter Enterprises' stock would drop if the wedding was suddenly canceled. And she also mentioned some pending deal with a pharmaceutical company that might fall through—"

"What exactly did she tell you about that deal?"

"No details," Carly replied. "She just said it might affect future profits."

"So you're doing this to protect Carpenter Enterprises?"

Carly frowned. "Not exactly. I'm doing it for my family, for Jenna and my father. But I suppose in a way they *are* Carpenter Enterprises. I've never had much to do with the company. But it's their life. Jenna's wanted to work there ever since she went to college. As for my father—well, after my mother's death, if it wasn't for Carpenter Enterprises, I think we would have lost my father, too. So, yes, I guess I am doing this to protect my father's company."

Loyalty. Holt could see it in her eyes, hear it in her voice. It was a quality he admired even though he'd taught himself long ago not to expect it. And yet, for a moment he hesitated. For just a moment he let himself think of what it might be like to have that kind of loyalty. Then he quickly reined his thoughts in. Marriage was the one part of the deal he'd made with Calvin Carpenter that he'd fought against. He'd agreed to marry Jenna only because Calvin had insisted. And he'd insisted on an escape clause in case Jenna backed out. Now that she had, Calvin couldn't technically hold him to an arranged marriage. "It's really not necessary for you to make this kind of sacrifice for Carpenter Enterprises. It's a strong company. The stock will survive. I'll talk to your father—"

"No." Carly moved around the desk to him and took his hands. "You don't understand. You haven't been up all night thinking it through. This marriage is very important to my father. It's his way of making sure that Carpenter Enterprises stays in the family...." For just a moment, as her sentence trailed off, Carly saw a flash of something in Holt's eyes. It was almost as if a little shutter had lifted and then slipped back into place. But whatever it was, she'd felt it right down to her toes.

"Your father wants grandchildren, Carly. Have you given any thought to that?"

For just a second Carly's mind went blank to everything but a brief, vivid image of Holt Cassidy and herself making love on a narrow bed in a very dark room. Suddenly she wasn't sure she could feel her legs. What she could feel was the heat flushing her cheeks. Licking her lips, she searched for words. After years of studying, reading, she had a lot of them stored away. Where were they? "Of course I've thought of it," she finally managed to say. *Brilliant*, she thought. Clearing her throat, she continued, "In every culture, especially in arranged marriages...well, that's what the marriage is arranged for. And even if that wasn't the intended goal in the beginning, it's the end result. Usually…"

The sentence faded away as Holt touched a hand to her cheek. "This may be your first proposal, but it's quite the nicest one—"

He was interrupted by the ringing of a phone. Fishing it out of his back pocket, he flipped it open. "Yes? No, don't do a thing. Carly's with me. We'll be right there."

Turning his attention to Carly, he asked, "Do you know who Jenna ran away with?"

"No. She refused to tell me. She was afraid if Dad found out, he'd find a way to stop her."

"That was your father on the phone. He's just received a ransom note that infers Jenna's been kidnapped."

2

NEITHER CARLY NOR HOLT spoke during the taxi ride to the Carpenter Building. But Carly's mind was racing. She stared straight ahead of her at the plastic partition that separated the cab driver from the passengers. Plastered against it, directly in her line of vision, was the license of the taxi driver. But Carly was looking right through it. Ever since Holt had hung up his cell phone, a knot of fear had settled in her stomach. And she'd always found that the best way to handle fear was logic. So while she'd waited for him to change into a suit, she'd gone over everything Jenna had told her when she'd broken the news of her elopement. Now Carly was replaying the scene once more.

A few minutes later she frowned. After twice reviewing every sentence of their conversation, Carly couldn't find a single thing in her sister's gestures or tone to contradict her conclusion that Jenna was truly in love and couldn't wait to elope with her lover.

That left her with two questions. Had the pair of lovers been kidnapped? Or had Jenna been duped by a fortune hunter? But that didn't quite make sense, either. If Jenna's lover had been after her money, he'd already struck pay dirt by convincing Jenna to marry him. Why would he then involve himself in a federal crime?

Carly felt the knot in her stomach tighten.

The taxi chugged along in fits and starts through the early morning traffic. The snow was falling in earnest now, big fat designer flakes that splatted against the window. But Holt paid them no heed. Ever since Calvin's frantic phone call, he'd been trying to figure out what was going on.

He didn't doubt for a minute that Carly was telling the truth as far as it had been told to her. She'd been convinced enough by her sister's romantic story of a last-minute elopement to offer herself as a substitute bride. But that didn't eliminate the possibility that Jenna might have lied to her sister and joined forces with her lover-blackmailer. Or Jenna could simply have been duped by her lover. A lover who wanted to extort money from Carpenter Enterprises and who was using her as a pawn. Either scenario explained why Jenna had kept the name of her lover and their destination a secret even from her sister.

Whatever the truth was, they had to find out who Jenna had "eloped" with and where the couple was. And they had to do it soon.

Carly was out of the taxi the moment it wedged itself into a space at the curb. After paying the driver, Holt followed her to the private family entrance. The Carpenter Building, twenty-five stories high, took up one snug corner of a busy Manhattan street. When Calvin had decided to move his headquarters from Wisconsin to New York, he'd also decided not to involve himself in the long daily commute to the suburbs. Instead, he'd turned the top floor of his new building into a spacious apartment containing living quarters for his family as well as his own private office. The rest of Carpenter Enterprises' offices filled the two floors below the penthouse.

Holt finally caught up to Carly at the elevator. She'd already used her key to open the doors, and within seconds they were shooting upward to the penthouse apartment. They found Calvin Carpenter, a large man with a shock of gray hair and a flair for the dramatic, pacing back and forth in his office, a paper clutched in his hand. "It's about time you got here!" he bellowed at them as he strode forward to envelop Carly in a fierce hug.

Holt extracted the paper from Calvin's fist and scanned the terse message.

Tit for tat! Give me the formula and research on Carly's tea project and your daughter will be returned in time for her wedding. Details at seven. Be in your office.

"I've already spoken with the security people. They're going to set up a trace on the phone and install a caller ID box. We're going to get your sister back!" Calvin squeezed Carly again. "And when I get my hands on the scum, I'll—"

"C'mon, Dad, let's sit down so we can figure this out," Carly said as she urged her father firmly into a seat on a nearby couch.

"What's to figure out?" Calvin protested.

"I don't think Jenna's been kidnapped," Carly replied.

Calvin shot up from his seat. "Well, she's gone! Her bed's not been slept in. And her clothes and suitcases are still here! I had our security people check her closet."

"She bought new clothes," Carly explained. "She

thought it would be too conspicuous if she left with a suitcase."

"Bought new clothes to be kidnapped?" He rested a hand on Carly's cheek. "You're not making sense, little girl. But don't you worry." He strode toward his desk and reached for the phone. "Now that you and Holt are here, I'm going to notify the police...the FBI."

Holt covered Calvin's hand on the receiver. "The more people who know, the more likely the press is to get hold of this."

"Let me see the note," Carly said. Once she'd scanned it, she frowned. "They're not asking for money. What's this 'Carly's tea project'?"

It was a moment before her father replied, and Carly didn't miss the look he exchanged with Holt first. "It's that mixture of herbs you sent home about a year ago. When you told me that the tribesmen on that island of yours were all living into their hundreds, I established a project to explore whether or not we could produce a tea that could have a positive effect on longevity. Holt here took charge of it once he came on board."

"Have you discovered anything yet?" Carly asked.

"Nothing definitive," Holt replied.

"Then why don't you just tell them that and turn over the formula?"

Calvin pounded his fist on the desk. "Never! The day that I give in to blackmail—"

"But, Dad," Carly interrupted, "those herbs are available to anyone who wants to fly to Manilai. They grow the stuff in irrigated fields."

"That's why we can't afford to have anyone find out about it," Calvin said. "If word gets around about where you found the herbs, every Tom, Dick and Harry will by flying out to that island, and Carpenter

Enterprises will no longer be able to offer Selkirk Pharmaceuticals exclusive rights to the research project."

Carly looked from her father to Holt. "Could you please explain?"

"Selkirk Pharmaceuticals did some of the preliminary research on the herbs for us. We're currently negotiating a deal that offers them the opportunity to continue work on the project in exchange for a future share of the profits," Holt said. "Of course, the research might not turn out to be as positive as the preliminary results, and in that case, Selkirk could be out some money. So far, two things have kept them at the bargaining table. The reputation of Carpenter Enterprises and the fact that we've been able to offer them exclusive rights to the 'formula.' The deal could fall apart if someone else gets hold of the herbs."

"And at this stage of the game, Selkirk could walk away simply because of the cancellation of the wedding this Friday," Calvin added. "They got skittish six months ago when I had my bypass done. If it hadn't been for Holt here, they would have walked." Sinking into his massive swivel chair, he fished through the bottom drawer of his desk and took out a cigar. He was striking a match when Carly walked over to take it out of his hands and blow it out.

"Your doctors have told you that stress and tobacco are a bad combination for you," she reminded him. "So you'd better hold off on that cigar until you hear what I have to say. I think the kidnapping's a hoax. Jenna has eloped."

"Eloped?" Calvin thundered, shooting up from his chair and leaning across his desk toward Carly. "First I get a ransom note demanding a formula that could mess up a very lucrative business deal, and now you're telling me that my Jenna has betrayed her family by eloping? Which is it, little girl?"

"Why don't you sit down?" Holt's voice was calm as he joined Carly at the desk. "If you'll give your heart a break and stop erupting like a geyser every few seconds, I'll tell you why Carly paid me a visit this morning at the crack of dawn."

And as soon as Calvin settled back into his chair, Holt proceeded to do just that. Much to Carly's surprise, her father listened without interrupting. What's more, he stayed in his seat.

Amazed, she turned to study Holt as he settled himself in a chair facing Calvin. He definitely had a knack for handling her father. If she'd been telling the story, Calvin would have been popping up out of his chair like a jack-in-the-box. As it was, the older man wasn't even reaching for his cigar.

Part of it was how quiet Holt himself had become, Carly decided. He was so different from her father. Calvin relied on dramatic gestures, bluster and bombast to drive his ideas home. Holt didn't seem to move at all. Perhaps the stillness of the man himself was contagious.

It wasn't just her father who had calmed down, she realized. Some of her own tension had eased, as well. Even Holt's voice seemed to have a soothing quality. It was deep, with a masculine kind of grittiness that Carly could almost feel brushing along her skin. Her gaze dropped to his hands where they rested on the arms of the chair. She remembered the roughness of his palm when it had been pressed against hers. She could almost imagine what it would feel like to have those callused hands move over her. They wouldn't soothe...

"So? Is it an elopement or a kidnapping?" Calvin asked suddenly.

With a start, Carly dragged her attention from Holt back to her father. "An elopement," she said firmly.

"Perhaps both," Holt suggested.

"Explain," Calvin said.

"Well, it occurs to me that there are two likely possibilities. Number one is that Carly's right. Jenna has eloped, but she's also cooperating with her lover to blackmail Carpenter Enterprises."

"No." Carly and Calvin spoke in unison, but this time it was Carly who erupted from her chair. "Jenna would never betray her family." Then, as she met Holt's eyes, it suddenly struck her that she was looking at the one person Jenna *had* betrayed. "I mean...well, I know you might find that very hard to believe. And it is true that this last-minute elopement puts the family in a bit of a bind...." *A bit of a bind? Lame, lame, lame!* Looking into Holt Cassidy's eyes for more than ten seconds seemed to have a paralyzing effect on her brain, Carly discovered. "Besides, Jenna didn't just take off. She spent most of last night making sure that I would take her place."

"Okay," Holt said calmly. "Another possibility is that someone with access to top secret information in the company has seduced Jenna, and she has no idea that she's being used as a pawn in this extortion scheme."

Calvin frowned. "So you're telling me that either my daughter or one of my most trusted employees is a traitor?"

While Carly listened to Holt paint the picture of a top level executive with either a grudge against Carpenter Enterprises or an immediate need for money, her mind was racing. As soon as he paused for a moment, she said, "There's another possibility." She began to pace. "The one thing I know for sure is that Jenna was in love with the man she ran away with last night. Neither one of you talked to her, watched her while she spoke. It wasn't a lie. This is my field of expertise. For the past two years, I've studied several young women as they went through the process of meeting and falling in love with the men they eventually married. And there's a way a woman looks when she's in love. Manhattan or Manilai, that look is universal. And I saw it on Jenna's face." Turning, Carly walked toward her father and Holt. "Just suppose someone else recognized that look on Jenna's face weeks ago? What if that someone made it a point to discover who Jenna was seeing and found out about the elopement plans? The blackmailer could be figuring that all we know is that Jenna's disappeared. He could believe that he can take advantage of our supposed ignorance to blackmail Carpenter Enterprises."

For a moment there was silence in the room. Holt was the first to break it. "It's possible," he finally said.

Calvin frowned, tapping his fingers on the desk. "It still means that one of my top executives could be a traitor." He reached for the phone. "I'll call them up here right now, and by all that's holy, I'll find out—"

Once more, Holt's hand covered Calvin's on the receiver. "And then everyone will know that Jenna has disappeared."

"Damn!" Calvin hung up the phone. "That leaves us caught between a rock and a hard place."

Holt's lips curved. "I think we have a little wiggling room. What we have to do is stall the blackmailer as long as we can. We'll pretend to go along with the de-

mands while we try to find out where Jenna has gone.
We can have our security people check the airlines, and
bus and train stations, and they can also try to find out
where Jenna met this person. As discreet as they were,
they must have left a trail. In the meantime, we tell
everyone that Jenna has a touch of the flu and that her
doctor has prescribed bed rest to ensure that she'll be
completely recovered for the wedding."

Calvin's smile spread slowly. "I like it. And just how
do we flush out the traitor?"

Carly watched in fascination as Holt hitched his
chair closer to her father's desk so they could discuss a
plan. She might not have been in the room for all the attention they paid to her. They were definitely two of a
kind, she decided. How could she have thought they
were different? Walking over, she placed her palms flat
on the surface of the desk and leaned toward them.
"And just what part do I get to play in this investigation?" she asked.

The two men turned in unison to look at her in surprise. "Why, you get to play the part you volunteered
for, little girl," Calvin explained with a smile. "You get
to substitute for your sister at all the social functions
we've got scheduled this week, starting with a special
company party today. Everyone is gathering at five in
the executive dining room for a private prewedding
celebration." Carly watched her father's smile fade
into a slight frown as his gaze wandered over the too
big sweatsuit she was wearing. "I hope you've got
something more suitable than that...outfit you've got
on. You'd better borrow something from your sister."

Carly opened her mouth to protest, but the two men
had already turned away to resume their discussion.
Typical, she thought as she pressed her lips together.

As much as she loved her father, Carly knew that he had a primitive view of men's and women's roles. In fact, Calvin Carpenter would fit right in with the tribesmen on Manilai who believed that women were limited to three functions in life: looking decorative, cooking and raising children. Preferably all at the same time.

Well, she thought as she studied the two men, if they thought they could get rid of her that easily, they'd find out they were wrong. Jenna was her sister, and Carly planned to play a very active role in finding her.

Suddenly, something Holt said caught her attention. He was talking about Tom Chadwick, the head of the research department at Carpenter Enterprises. Married with two children, Tom had moved from Wisconsin to New York with Calvin eight years ago. He was almost a member of the family, and Holt was putting him at the top of his suspect list because Tom was unhappy that Holt had been put in charge of Carly's tea project. Carly had her mouth open, ready to defend Tom, but her father beat her to it.

All during Calvin's emotional and long-winded harangue, Holt sat quietly in his chair. The moment Calvin ran out of steam, Holt calmly named two other people. Danny Gallagher in accounting, who'd dated Jenna a few times and who might, therefore, have had some dreams of becoming Calvin's son-in-law. And Mark Miller, a VP who'd been with the company a year longer than Holt and who might have had his sights set on eventually stepping into Calvin's shoes.

Once more Calvin leaped into the breach to defend his employees, but this time Carly wasn't tempted to join him. It had suddenly occurred to her that if they wanted to figure out who was behind the extortion attempt, Holt was doing exactly what they all should be doing. Looking at the facts with an objective eye. Calvin felt all his employees were family. But that didn't mean they weren't capable of betrayal.

Wasn't Jenna a prime example of that? Once more Carly's eyes shifted to Holt. He was just sitting there, quietly letting Calvin's torrent of words pour over him. Moments ago, she'd been ready to join her father in the attack. Hadn't her gut reaction been anger when she'd heard Tom Chadwick's name? And now? Well, she wasn't sure what she was feeling. But she had to let him know that he wasn't alone. The second her father paused to take a breath, Carly said, "Holt is right. Listen to him."

"He's accusing family, little girl. Tom, Danny, Mark—none of them would do something like this!"

"Maybe not," Carly said. "But if we want to get Jenna back safely, we have to consider all the possibilities. Besides, family members betray each other all the time. It happens in every culture." She didn't dare look at Holt. She couldn't bear to mention Jenna. "When a married woman is murdered, more often than not it's by her husband. Even in biblical times, the seeds of betrayal flourished best in families. Look at Cain and Abel, for heaven's sake!"

For a moment, Calvin was silent, his eyes narrowing as he studied his daughter. Then he shifted his gaze to Holt. "Smart girl. She's got all those degrees after her name. Could be she has a point."

"Well, if I've made it, I'll leave the two of you to sort out the details while I try to find something more appropriate to wear for the party this afternoon." Without waiting for a reply, Carly picked up her backpack, turned and walked to the door.

Even as it clicked shut behind her, she was headed toward Jenna's bedroom rather than her own. And not just to change her clothes.

There might be something in the room that would shed some light on the identity of Jenna's lover or at least on their honeymoon destination.

Opening the door, she stepped inside. The pale wintry light struggling through the window did little to relieve the darkness. Carly couldn't even make out Priscilla, Jenna's cat, until she flicked on the light switch.

"Mmmrow," Priscilla remarked as she rose slowly and regally from her position at the foot of the bed.

"I'll bet you know where Jenna is," Carly said in an accusing tone as she joined Priscilla on the bed.

"Mmmrow," Priscilla replied as she settled herself again.

Absently, Carly reached over to run her hand over the cat. "I should have made her tell me. I can certainly understand her determination to keep it a secret from Dad after that fiasco in high school." It had been years since Carly had thought of the incident. They'd been in Wisconsin at the time. Jenna had been a junior in high school, and she'd fallen head over heels for a young man who was about to graduate. They'd wanted to get married. The moment Calvin had found out about it, he'd had a fit. And then he'd taken action. To this day, Carly didn't know all the details, but a week after graduation, the young man and his family had moved away.

Jenna had cried her heart out for weeks. It was one of the many times Carly had wished desperately for her mother. Nothing she'd said or done had seemed to comfort Jenna. It was the longest summer of Carly's life, but eventually Jenna's broken heart had mended, and she'd gone back to school in the fall.

"If only I'd pushed her a little harder to tell me." She glanced down at Priscilla and gave her a pat. "If only cats could talk...." Carly sighed. It was too late for if-onlys now. If she wanted to locate Jenna, she'd have to find another way. Rising, she moved to the dresser and began to methodically open each drawer.

In the top one, she found a passport. Waving it at Priscilla, she said, "This narrows it down to the North American continent." The next three drawers contained neat rows of lingerie, sweaters, panty hose and a box filled with matchbooks. Carly had the bottom drawer almost closed when the thought finally registered. Jenna didn't smoke. Carefully she sorted the matchbooks into two piles. One advertised Bistro 720, the other a dance club called Club Metro. Carly couldn't recall ever being to either of them with her family. Could they be souvenirs of places Jenna had been with her lover? Frowning, Carly scooped up the piles, replaced them carefully and closed the drawer. Why else would Jenna start a collection of matches?

Frustrated, Carly planted her hands on her hips. Why hadn't she asked Jenna more questions? She would have if she hadn't been so distracted by thoughts of Holt Cassidy.

It was then that realization slammed into her. Very slowly she met her own eyes in the mirror above the dresser.

Holt hadn't answered her proposal.

She'd used every argument she could think of to convince the man to marry her, and he hadn't even replied.

Surprise, surprise, she thought as she studied her reflection. She wasn't nearly as pretty as Jenna. Nor as tall. Jenna's eyes were dark brown. Her own were amber. Jenna had long dark hair that fell in a smooth curve to her shoulders. Her own hair was honey-colored in a South Seas light, a sort of streaked wheat color in the less flattering, wintry light of Manhattan. And she favored a short, practical cut.

Carly wrinkled her nose at the woman staring back at her. In almost every way she was a smaller, paler, less dramatic version of her younger sister. She must have been absolutely insane to think Holt Cassidy would want to marry her instead of her sister.

Placing her hands flat on the top of the dresser, she leaned toward the mirror to get a closer look. Her eyes were clear and focused, the pupils undilated. She wasn't foaming at the mouth.

But she was an anthropologist, not a psychiatrist. What did she know about madness? The closest she'd come to an insane person was attending a theatrical presentation of *Jane Eyre*. And the woman staring back at her from the mirror didn't look as if she had to be locked away in an attic. At least, not yet.

A more likely diagnosis was that she was suffering from caffeine withdrawal. She'd barely had three sips at Holt's apartment.

Pushing herself away from the mirror, Carly began to pace. From all of her observations on the island, falling in love inevitably led to a state of euphoria. That's why she'd known that Jenna was truly in love. Had her sister's condition rubbed off on her? Had she been looking at the whole idea of marrying Holt Cassidy through some cockeyed, unfocused, rose-colored glasses?

There was only one way to find out. Moving to the

bed, Carly fished the note cards out of her backpack and shuffled through them. She was searching not for the one she'd used with Holt, but the one she'd used to convince herself to go along with Jenna's plan.

Sitting down, she read the neat printing. She'd agreed to propose to Holt for three reasons. Number one, because it would be convenient. After all, she'd come back to Manhattan with the goal of finding herself a husband. And Jenna had dropped Holt right into her lap, eliminating the need for the whole selection process. Some of the young women on the island had taken months to find the right man.

And marrying Holt Cassidy would allow her to kill two birds with one stone. She not only got a husband but got to help her family, too.

Carly drew in a deep breath and let it out. She *didn't* have bats in her belfry. Marrying Holt Cassidy truly *was* a good idea. Thoughtfully, she zipped the card back into her bag. There were still problems to be faced. What if Holt was right and Jenna was the victim of an elaborate con game aimed at extorting money from Carpenter Enterprises? Then the whole idea of becoming a substitute bride might be a moot point. If they found Jenna before Friday, she might be perfectly willing to walk down the aisle with Holt Cassidy herself.

"No." Carly sprang up from the bed, surprised at how much vehemence she heard in the one explosive syllable.

"Mmmrow?" The question came from Priscilla.

"I don't *know* what's the matter." Carly whirled to face the cat. "If Jenna finds out that her elopement is a hoax and she still wants to marry Holt, I should be...relieved." The problem was that the little tug of pain that was pulling at her heart was not relief. And it wasn't the first time she'd experienced it, either. She'd felt the same little tug in Holt's apartment when she'd had to tell him about Jenna's elopement. Then she'd felt it again a few moments ago in Calvin's office when she'd tried to explain how loyal Jenna was.

Loyal to everyone except Holt.

Carly walked to the mirror and met her own eyes squarely. "There's no need to change your plan. Jenna could come back a happily married woman. If not…well, there's no way to solve that problem until we find Jenna." Carly began to pace. A good starting place to find clues about Jenna's disappearance might be the company party. Holt's top three suspects would be there. Carly didn't believe for a minute that they were involved, but one of them might have noticed something. And then there were those matches from the restaurant and the dance club where Jenna might have been meeting her lover. She could visit them and see if anyone could identify her sister.

But in the meantime, she had another problem. Holt Cassidy. It was then, as she turned and paced back to the dresser, that she noticed the framed photograph. Lifting it, she studied the picture of her father and Jenna and Holt Cassidy. Jenna was laughing, and Calvin was smiling, his arm around his daughter. Holt, his expression sober, stood a little apart from them. Alone.

Carly ran a finger slowly along the side of his face and along his shoulder. She'd always been a sucker for loners and strays. In college, her room had eventually turned into a menagerie of abandoned pets. Hamsters, gerbils, tropical fish. She'd even given refuge to a python, but only temporarily. A snake that ate other live animals whole was just a little too dangerous for her taste.

In fact, come to think of it, the python reminded her a lot of Holt. Both of them were incredibly self-contained and competent. And dangerous. But she hadn't been able to abandon that python until she'd found a home for it in a zoo. And there was something, some instinct deep inside of her, that didn't want Holt to be alone, either.

The difference was that she'd understood the python. The snake had been motivated by hunger and survival. But she didn't have a clue about what motivated Holt Cassidy. Except for money. Would the shares in Carpenter Enterprises be enough to convince him to marry her?

Carly studied Holt's picture, the strong features, the inscrutable eyes. If he thought he could take over as CEO of Carpenter Enterprises and get those shares without having to marry a Carpenter daughter, he'd cancel the wedding in a second, Carly decided. And Jenna's desertion gave him the perfect bargaining chip.

If there was one thing that Carly believed in, it was facing the truth. And the truth was that if she wanted Holt to marry her, she'd have to *do* something. And she shouldn't be surprised by that. Didn't her research support the fact that during most of the courting rituals on the island of Manilai, the women called the shots?

The difficulty was in trying to picture any woman calling the shots with Holt Cassidy. And the one thing she couldn't afford to do was underestimate how dangerous he was to her. There was that incredible effect he seemed to have on her equilibrium. It was one thing to look at his photo and think logically. It was an entirely different matter when she had to face him in per-

son. He'd only touched her twice, in the most casual of
ways. And both times her nerve endings had sparked
like hot, naked wires.

And then she recalled that moment in his apartment
when she'd taken his hands in hers and looked into his
eyes. Even now, she could recall each and every sensation as clearly as if it were happening again. The tiny
click at the back of her brain that shut off access to rational thought, the shortness of breath, the funny
weakness in her knees, and woven through it all an exciting feeling of anticipation.

Taking a deep breath, Carly carefully lifted her finger from the photo where it had been resting on Holt
Cassidy's shoulder. Very interesting symptoms. She'd
have to remember to record them on a note card. And
in the meantime, she'd have to take great care not to let
Holt Cassidy know the effect he had on her. If she was
going to set out to attract him, she would be playing
with fire. And unless she took great care to hold her
own with him, she might very well get consumed in
the flames.

Carly set the photo back on the dresser and faced
herself in the mirror. "So, just how do you intend to attract a man like Holt Cassidy? The brilliance of your
Aristotelian logic was a complete bust. What's next?"

Carly frowned at herself. The truth was that everything she knew about attracting a man could fit on half
of one of her three-by-five note cards. And the history
of her love life could fill the other half. Unlike Jenna,
she'd never met her Romeo in high school. And after
her mother's death, there hadn't been much time. Calvin had been lost in his grief, and Jenna had needed a
mother. By the time she'd gotten to college, she'd been
four years older than most of her classmates. Boys

looked on her as an older sister, a confidante. The one affair she'd had in graduate school with her psychology professor certainly hadn't been a confidence builder. She'd been too naive to realize until it was too late that she'd merely been his annual spring fling.

Pushing herself away from the dresser, she turned back to Priscilla. "I don't suppose you'd like to share a few of your manhunting...excuse me, cat-hunting secrets?"

Priscilla didn't bother to look up. All her attention was focused on cleaning her left paw.

"Even *I* know that personal hygiene is a step in the right direction. But I was hoping for something just a little more inventive. Like a miracle, maybe. Or a couple good flicks of a fairy godmother's wand!" She was on her way to join Priscilla on the bed when a thought suddenly struck her and she stopped short in her tracks. "Wait a minute! What am I thinking of? Where are my brains?" She pointed a finger at the cat. "You know, if I don't find a way to get a regular supply of caffeine, I may start to flatline."

Priscilla continued to clean her paws.

"I know a lot about how to attract a man. A whole lot." Carly spoke the words aloud. Hearing them made her more confident. "In fact, I'm writing a book on it. I brought all of my research with me. Two boxes of note cards. Of course, the island of Manilai isn't Manhattan. I'll have to adapt some of the customs." She paused at the foot of the bed to address Priscilla directly. "But if there's one thing that I've learned from studying different cultures, it's that there are common threads that seem to run through all of them." Warming to her theme, Carly began to pace again. "The island of Manhattan may be located in a different hemisphere and on a different ocean, but men and women here have the same needs and desires as they do on Manilai. The same needs and desires that they had in Shakespeare's day and even in Biblical times. Food, shelter and the desire to find a mate are pretty universal. Otherwise we wouldn't be here, would we?"

Priscilla didn't reply. She merely favored Carly with a rather superior glance.

Carly studied the cat with a thoughtful frown. "Well, it's a little different for you. You don't have all these cultural pressures urging you to mate for life." Turning, Carly moved to the closet. "The one thing the women on Manilai do when they start to notice men is pay particular attention to their clothes. Actually, they seem to wear fewer of them." Her hand seemed to move of its own accord to a red wool suit. "Now, I'm not saying that I'm going to dress up in a sarong and dance half-naked in the moonlight. And I'm certainly not going to put a ring through my nose." Pausing at Jenna's dresser, she pulled open a drawer. "I suppose the Manhattan translation of that is earrings. And they wear a lot of flowers, too. Some of Jenna's French perfume ought to do the trick."

For the second time, she leaned toward the mirror to study her reflection. "They do something to darken their eyes and paint their cheeks, too. I guess makeup's pretty universal."

"Mmmrow!"

"You know, come to think of it, you cats have it pretty easy," Carly said. "You only have to concentrate on body language. I have a whole pack of note cards on that topic."

3

OUTSIDE THE WALL of windows in the executive dining room, darkness had fallen, and the wind whistled, pummeling snow against the pane of glass. Inside, the room was filled with the scent of burning candles and fresh flowers, and above it the aroma of hot food. At the edge of a raised platform, string musicians played, their sound muted at times by excited conversation, laughter and the clink of glasses.

Holt held himself apart from the other revelers, sipping a glass of champagne and using the time to observe. At least that was what he told himself he was doing as he let his gaze sweep the room. But there was a part of him that was simply waiting. For someone to make a betraying move?

He switched his attention to Calvin, who stood a few feet away talking to his three top executives, Tom Chadwick, Mark Miller and Danny Gallagher, the men that he and Calvin had spent more than an hour discussing. Each had a possible motive for revenge against Carpenter Enterprises. Just then, Calvin's booming laughter erupted, momentarily drowning out the other party noises. The men joined in, perfectly at ease.

Holt hadn't expected anything different. If one of them *was* involved with Jenna's disappearance, he wouldn't want to draw attention to himself in any way.

He switched his gaze back to the line of people who had already begun to gather at the tables laden with food. A few couples were dancing on the platform. Everything seemed normal. No one had even remarked on Jenna's absence yet. The truth was, Holt didn't expect to find out anything at this party. He was just marking time. So why did he feel keyed up? It had to be frustration. The blackmail note had arrived almost eight hours ago, and so far the firm's security people had come up with nothing.

Then he looked back, as he already had several times, at the doors to Calvin's private elevator. And suddenly it occurred to him—he was waiting for Carly to arrive.

When the doors slid silently open and she stepped through them, all Holt could do was stare.

Surprise was the first emotion he identified as he watched the woman in the red suit walk toward him. For several seconds he hadn't even recognized her. Not until she'd met his eyes and he'd felt the same elemental pull he'd felt when he'd first taken her hand. This was Carly. Carly, whose hair looked mussed as if some man had just run his fingers through it. Carly, whose skirt stopped several inches above her knees and whose legs seemed to go on...and on...

Holt had taken a step forward before he suddenly realized that she wasn't walking toward him. Instead, she'd veered to join the group of men surrounding her father. Tom Chadwick leaned down to kiss her cheek, Mark Miller gave her a friendly hug. But Danny Gallagher swung her off her feet, then kissed her full on the mouth. And Carly responded with a delighted laugh.

Holt stopped himself from moving toward the

group, but some of the champagne spilled from the glass he was gripping, and his other hand formed a fist at his side. It was then that he began to recognize the other emotion warring with the surprise he was feeling. Jealousy? A part of him wanted to deny it flatly. But there was no denying the fact that another part of him wanted to walk over there and pull Carly bodily away from the group of men. And it was clearly relief he felt as Calvin took his older daughter's hand and tucked it protectively in his arm.

Taking another sip of his wine, Holt studied Carly. Although the woman standing a few feet from him was a sharp right turn from the elf in the oversize sweats who had proposed to him earlier that day, Holt knew for a fact that it wasn't the change in clothes or hair that had triggered the flood of emotions in him. It was Carly herself.

Why? he wondered with a frown. From the first, she hadn't been what he'd expected. The woman he'd met at dinner last night hadn't fit the image he'd formed in his mind of the serious intellectual, wandering through academia wearing bulky clothes and sensible, square-toed shoes.

His glance wandered from her face down the neat, slender body and incredibly long legs to the high-heeled, strappy sandals she was wearing. Even as he watched, she balanced precariously on one foot and rubbed the other behind her ankle. Who in the world was she? And more important, why hadn't he yet refused her proposal?

Why was he hesitating, deliberating? He could have broached the subject with Calvin the moment Carly left the office. And if he told himself that he'd avoided the topic because he didn't want to add to Calvin's distress over Jenna's apparent elopement, it would be a lie. Long ago he'd learned not to let emotion interfere when it came to his own survival. It was Jenna's name that was on the agreement that he and Calvin had signed. He wasn't under any obligation to accept Carly in Jenna's place. And yet he hadn't brought up the subject to Calvin.

On the other hand, it wasn't in his nature to act impulsively, either, Holt thought as he watched Carly shift her weight to her other foot. He glanced down at her shoes. Slowly the corners of his mouth lifted. She wasn't comfortable in those sandals. Perhaps he hadn't been so far off about the square-toed, sensible shoes, after all. For the first time since he'd entered the executive dining room, Holt began to relax.

The sharp staccato sound of a gavel being struck on a table brought Holt's attention back to Calvin. Keeping Carly's arm tucked in his, Calvin drew her onto the platform with the dancers. Then he turned and waved at Holt to join them.

By the time Holt reached the table, the older man had a champagne bottle high in the air. "Attention! Hear, hear," he shouted.

In a moment, the music stopped and the conversation faded. "You all know why we're having this celebration today." He waved the bottle. "To toast the bride and groom. But Jenna is feeling a little under the weather. A touch of the flu, according to the doctor. And he's ordered her off her feet so she can be back on them for the wedding on Friday."

As Calvin talked, Holt scanned the crowd. The expressions on people's faces ranged from mild surprise to polite concern.

"And until Jenna's fully recovered," Calvin continued, "Carly here, as maid of honor, will be standing in for her. Now the toast! To the bride and groom!"

"Hear! Hear!" The cheer from the crowd was mixed with the sounds of champagne corks popping. Immediately, the string quartet began to play again.

Calvin was topping off Carly's glass when a young woman joined them on the platform. "Did Jenna have any message for me?" she asked.

Carly turned to find herself looking at a woman with medium brown hair pulled back into a chignon. She wore a faultlessly neat gray suit and wire-rimmed glasses. "You must be...?"

"Jenna's secretary, Susan Masterson." Susan held out her hand. "Perhaps I should go up and see her? I'm sure she'll have instructions."

Carly smiled and squeezed the hand she was holding. "The doctor gave her something to make her sleep. I'll talk to her first thing in the morning and let you know. In the meantime, I'm sure her instructions would be for you to enjoy the party."

"Yes. Fine." Susan gave her a brief nod before she stepped down from the platform.

"Nicely done, little girl," Calvin said.

"I'll have to know more about Jenna's schedule by tomorrow morning. Otherwise, Miss Masterson might become suspicious."

Calvin patted his daughter's arm. "Don't you worry, pumpkin. Holt will handle everything."

Over her dead body, Carly thought as she glanced over her father's shoulder to where Holt was standing, scanning the crowd. She'd avoided looking at him ever since her eyes had connected with his when she'd first stepped off the elevator.

Something had happened in that instant, although

she wasn't sure what. All she knew was that the sounds of the party, the music, the hum of conversation, everything had suddenly died down. For one moment, all she'd been aware of was Holt.

It was as if time had stopped. And that only happened in movies—like in *West Side Story*, when Tony met Maria at the school gym. Carly knew from her study of physics that time could never stand still in real life. So she'd forced herself to take a deep breath, and somehow she'd managed to shift her gaze away from Holt Cassidy's eyes. A moment later she'd smelled flowers...burning candles...food. Seconds after that, she'd heard the string quartet playing, and somehow her feet had carried her to her father's side. If she could just manage to exercise a little control around Holt, she was going to be able to hold her own. She was almost sure of it.

Suddenly she winced and shifted her weight to her right foot. And in the future, she was going to wear more comfortable shoes. Jenna's sandals were killing her. The one advantage the women on her island had was that they never had to wear high heels. They went barefoot.

"Carly?"

She turned to smile at Mark Miller. He'd worked for Carpenter Enterprises less than two years, and she'd only met him a few times. He'd struck her then as serious-minded, and so far she hadn't changed her opinion.

"Jenna isn't..." He paused to smile slightly. "What I mean is...well, has she changed her mind about the wedding?"

Carly's smile widened. "No, it's definitely the flu,

not a case of cold feet. Unless you know something I don't?"

"Nothing except that Holt Cassidy seems like an odd match for your sister," Tom Chadwick said as he joined them.

"Odd in what way?" Carly asked.

Tom shrugged. "Jenna's so outgoing, like your father. Cassidy's...well, he's reserved, to say the least."

"He's downright secretive, if you ask me," Danny Gallagher said as he hopped up on the platform. "But he'll probably do a hell of a job running the company. And we—" he paused to raise his glass in a toast to his two colleagues "—will just have to get used to a new management style." Then, setting his empty glass on the tray of a passing waiter, he took Carly's hand. Now, if you'll excuse me, gentlemen, I'm going to steal the maid of honor for a dance."

"I'm afraid you'll have to wait your turn, Gallagher," Holt said as he took Carly's hand from Danny's and tucked it into his. "I believe I have first claim on my stand-in bride."

Carly had sensed Holt's approach even before he'd spoken, so she'd had time to brace herself before he pulled her into his arms on the dance floor. Already she could feel the warmth spreading from where his fingers were linked with hers. Quick. She had to say something. Anything.

Meeting his eyes, she asked, "What if the stand-in bride doesn't want to dance? My feet are killing me."

"I noticed. And I think Gallagher had some fancy stepping in mind. I've heard he takes dance lessons."

"Danny?" Carly asked in surprise.

"This could be the third time today I've saved your life."

Carly's eyes narrowed as she studied him closely. The corners of his mouth were definitely curving upward. "That was a joke, wasn't it?"

Holt's grin was wry. "I'll have to work on my timing."

What he didn't have to work on was his smile, Carly thought. It was a killer, and it was definitely linked to what she was feeling. With one part of her mind, she tried hard to concentrate on analyzing the sensations rolling through her. With the other part of her mind, she simply felt them. Because it was starting to happen again. She was starting to lose her train of thought. There was something that she had to ask Holt and…it was just out of reach. And then there was the warmth radiating from his touch. Not the hot, zingy, almost electric sensation she'd felt before. No, this was more like a thick liquid moving through her, turning her knees slowly to jelly. And she couldn't feel her feet at all.

For a second she wished desperately for her note cards. But using them would be problematic. Holt had her hand trapped in his. And she was vividly aware of the roughness of his palms.

It was so interesting. And though only their hands touched, she was also very aware of the firmness of his body, his heat. So close. What would happen, she wondered, if she leaned forward and brought her body into full contact with his?

As if in answer to her question, Holt released one of her hands and used his own to draw her closer. When his thigh brushed against her, Carly felt the torrid arrow of heat shoot to her center like a missile seeking its target.

Run was her first impulse.

Stay was her second.

Much later, she would rationalize that it was the shoes that kept her right where she was. They were definitely not made for running. But as she gazed into Holt Cassidy's eyes, a question drifted through her mind. Was it pythons or cobras who hypnotized their prey just before they struck?

HE WAS DANCING with two women, Holt finally decided. There was the intellectual, minus the baggy sweater and sensible shoes, who'd been looking at him with those wide amber eyes only moments ago as if he were some laboratory rat she was observing for an experiment. And then there was the woman he was looking at now, whose breath caught on a hitch and who trembled when he simply ran his thumb across her knuckles.

Both fascinated him. He admired the incredible intelligence in the one and the equally incredible innocence in the other. It suddenly struck him that he wanted both of them.

And desire for either one of them was a luxury he simply couldn't afford. Finding Jenna, her supposed lover and the blackmailer had to be his first priority. And then he would deal with Carly and her marriage proposal.

"Did you learn anything from talking to Chadwick, Miller and Gallagher?" Holt asked.

For a moment Carly didn't answer. Holt thought he might have to repeat the question. Then suddenly she blinked. "How did you...? Was it that obvious that I was..."

"Grilling them for clues?" Holt asked. "No. You appeared to be making proper party small talk. But I figured you wouldn't waste the opportunity."

"No." Carly sighed. "But I thought it would be easy, more like my research. I'd just ask questions, and they'd answer. But being a detective is easier in books. I mean, I just can't come right out and ask them, 'Did you seduce Jenna? Are you blackmailing my father?' I can't even ask them if Jenna was acting strangely—like she was in love. Because they would have assumed that she was in love with you..." Carly's hand tightened on his shoulder. "I'm sorry. I..."

"Don't be. I knew Jenna wasn't in love with me."

Carly dropped her gaze to Holt's tie. "Well, I can't believe she was in love with any of *them*, either."

"No," Holt agreed. "But they could be working with the man Jenna eloped with."

Carly glanced over to see Mark and Danny still in conversation with her father. Out of the corner of her eye she saw Tom headed toward the buffet table. "It's still hard for me to believe that one of them would betray my father."

"And yet you came to my defense in your father's office. Why?"

Carly met Holt's eyes. "Because I want to get my sister back, and I don't think we should overlook any possibility. Just as soon as I get hold of Jenna's schedule, I'll have a much better idea of where she might have met her mystery lover, and then—"

"Carly, your father and I appreciate your desire to help out. But we've decided that it's best if you confine your movements to the private quarters for the next few days. I'll see that you get a copy of Jenna's schedule, and we can meet tomorrow morning to discuss it."

Carly stopped dancing and removed her hands from

Holt's. "I'm not a child. You can't simply send me to my room. It's my sister who's—"

"Exactly," Holt said, taking her arm and drawing her to the edge of the dance floor. They stopped next to the musicians, and Holt spoke so softly that she had to rely on lipreading to catch his next words. "Whoever this blackmailer is, he hasn't hesitated to use your sister as a pawn. I want to make sure he doesn't use you next."

Carly opened her mouth and then shut it. What he said was logical enough to send a sliver of fear racing up her spine. Still, it wasn't fear that stopped her from arguing with him. It was the look in his eyes. They'd been lit with amusement a few moments ago, and now they looked like a rain forest in the middle of a deluge. Any words she might summon up would be wasted on him now. Years of living with her father had taught her the futility of banging her head against a brick wall. Besides, actions spoke louder than words. She'd just have to prove to him that he needed her help to find Jenna and the blackmailer.

Summoning up a smile, she said, "I don't suppose any of those silver urns over on the buffet table have coffee in them."

She had the satisfaction of seeing Holt's lips twitch as he replied, "Not a chance. You still have your instant, don't you?"

Carly wrinkled her nose. "Yes, but it's tricky. Dad's very good at smelling it on my breath. I hate to upset him with everything else that's..." Carly let the sentence trail off as she spotted the tall, heavily built man in the cowboy hat making his way through the guests toward her father. Sam Waterman ran one of the country's largest soft-drink manufacturing companies, and his rivalry with her father had gone on ever since she could remember. And it wasn't just business. "What in the world is Sam Waterman doing at this party? He and my dad almost fought a duel once over my mother."

Holt's eyes narrowed as he followed the direction of her gaze. "Your father invited him."

"Not in this lifetime." But even as she said the words, Carly saw her father laugh and slap Sam on the back. Immediately, she whirled to face Holt. "I couldn't be more surprised if I found an espresso machine in my father's office. What's going on?"

Holt shrugged. "Ever since his bypass surgery, Calvin has been reaching out to people, trying to mend old fences."

"If I had a list of suspects—" Carly began.

"Sam's been in Atlanta for the past week. He flew in this morning for the party, and he plans to stay for the wedding. One of Carpenter Enterprises' security people has been assigned to watch his hotel room."

Carly's eyes widened. "I'm impressed. But if I don't have to go back to my room just yet and hide under the covers, I think I'll go over and pay my respects to Mr. Waterman."

Carly wandered over and made polite small talk with her father's nemesis for a few minutes. But what she really intended to do was get lost in the crowd. Not too quickly, though. The last thing she wanted to do was alarm Holt with a sudden disappearing act. She could have kicked herself for not having thought of it sooner. But with everyone at the party, the business offices on the floor below would be empty. It was the perfect time to search Jenna's desk. At the very least, there had to be a day planner and a Rolodex.

If she'd been thinking straight, she'd have taken the elevator down before she'd even come to the party. But she'd been totally focused on dressing up to capture Holt Cassidy's attention. Well, she'd certainly accomplished that goal. Carly didn't even have to glance over her shoulder to know that Holt still had her in view. She could feel his gaze on her like an electric current skimming along her nerve endings. Her new goal was to become invisible so that she could do a little uninterrupted investigating.

Pausing to chat with some of the secretaries who wanted to send their best wishes to Jenna, Carly gauged the distance to the nearest exit door. It would be less conspicuous to use the stairs than the elevator.

But it seemed to take hours to make her way through the crowd. Before turning the knob, she gave the room one last, casual scan. She could pick out Sam Waterman because of his hat. And her father because of his booming laugh. But blessedly, there was no sign of Holt. Taking a deep breath, she slipped through the door and let it swing shut behind her. The sounds of the party dimmed, and the air was cool against her skin. A naked bulb overhead barely illuminated the steep stairs and the narrow landing below. Taking off her shoes, she carried them in one hand, reached for the railing with the other and began her descent.

Five steps down, the light went out, pitching the stairwell into darkness. Carly stopped short and listened. Had the party noises picked up for a second there? Suddenly she felt a blow between her shoulder blades. Her hand was torn free from the railing and she hurtled forward.

Carly felt as if she were falling into a black hole. Her right foot came down hard on a stair and the pain of

the impact was still singing up her leg when her left
foot smacked against another. And then she was stum-
bling across solid ground. The landing. Her hands
slammed into the cement wall seconds before her body
did.

For a moment, she clung to the wall, blessedly
numb, and then the sensations battered through her.
The stinging in her hands, the burning in her throat.
Had she screamed? The pounding pain in her feet, her
legs. And finally the rolling fear. Someone had shoved
her. Who? Why?

Though her instinct was to push herself away from
the wall and try to escape, Carly forced herself to stay
still. And listen. She might not be alone. The person
who'd pushed her could be a few feet away. Perhaps
only inches. Waiting...

Even as she felt the bubble of hysteria rise, she
shoved it down and forced herself to take a deep, silent
breath. On the count of ten, she released it. Then she
breathed in again. Ten seconds passed, then twenty.
She couldn't hear a thing.

Then a sound drifted down from above. The soft
scrape of metal against metal, a crescendo in the noise
of the party.

Then silence.

To ward off a fresh wave of panic, Carly made herself concentrate on the coldness of the cement against
her hands, the roughness of it against her cheek. She
counted off twenty seconds before she began to inch
her way along the wall, one step at a time, until she
reached the railing.

Her eyes had grown used to the darkness. Below her
she could just make out the dim glow of the exit sign.
The door to the twenty-third floor. When she made

herself glance behind her, she saw nothing but darkness. Turning back, she fixed her gaze on the sign. She
had two choices. She could walk down slowly, step by
step, waiting for another shove. Or... Without another
thought, Carly launched herself down the stairs,
grabbed the knob, pulled and raced into the warmth of
the twenty-third floor. For a moment she stood, staring
at the maze of partitioned offices. Only a few work-
stations were lit, but the light seemed bright after the
darkness of the stairs.

Suddenly her anger rose up to war with her fear.
Turning, she pushed open the door and flipped on the
light. The stairwell and the landing above were empty.
With her hand still gripping the door, she hesitated. It
was useless to go back up to the party. She didn't have
any idea who had pushed her.

Or why. She recalled Holt's claim that whoever was
using Jenna as a pawn might not stop there. What if he
was right and the blackmailer was coming after her
next? Suppressing a fresh wave of fear, she forced herself to think.

One thing was very clear. She couldn't tell her father
or Holt about the incident or they'd have her under
house arrest, quick as a blink. No, she'd have to handle
the threat by herself. Because no one, especially not
some cowardly blackmailer, was going to prevent her
from finding her sister! Turning, she strode through
the maze of cubicles to the far end of the floor, where
Jenna's name was painted on a door.

She paused in front of what she supposed was Susan
Masterson's desk. It was as neat as the woman herself.
Not so much as a stray pencil marred its clean surface.
Not even a blotter or an appointment book. Carly was

reaching for the handle of the top drawer when she heard the noise.

Just the faintest whisper of a paper turning.

Heart hammering, she took a quick step toward the office door. Jenna? No, it couldn't be. She stopped, grateful that she was in her stocking feet, and took a slow, steadying breath. Whoever had attacked her on the stairs had gone back up to the party. She was sure of that. Then she noticed that the door was open a crack. As she moved carefully toward it, another paper whispered. Straining, Carly peered through the opaque glass, trying to make out something. A shadow. Anything.

When she reached the door, she planted her palms against it and shoved it hard. The room was empty. Carly hurried toward the desk, only to be grabbed and pulled backward until she was pressed flat against the wall. Before she could scream, a hand clamped against her mouth. Another pinned her hands above her head.

"Carly?"

The words were spoken in a whisper, but Carly knew it was Holt. He released her almost instantly, but in that small snatch of time, she experienced exactly what it was like to have Holt's body pressed fully against hers. For a second, every inch of her had been aware of the length of his thigh, the sharp angle of his hip, the quick beat of his heart. And for just a second, a thousand little pinpricks of pleasure had exploded at each and every contact point.

The explosions continued, even after he drew back a little. It was chemistry, Carly told herself. And it was just her luck that chemistry had never been her best subject. To keep herself upright, she tried to recall the periodic table. It flashed into her mind, then faded right out again when he slid his hand from her lips to rest for a moment along the side of her throat. She had to move, get away. But she didn't dare. There was no way to get past him without touching him again. A smart woman didn't jump willingly into a volcano once she knew it was there.

Holt said nothing as he studied her for one brief, humming moment. Then, very slowly, he dropped his hand to his side and took two steps back. He'd barely touched her, but for just an instant he'd felt every slim line and curve of her pressed against him. It was only the briefest of contacts, and yet it was enough to have desire twisting like a rusty knife in his gut.

He could see a trace of fear in her eyes. And she was right to be afraid. She didn't have any idea of what a man like him was capable of. He still said nothing as he clenched his fingers into fists at his side. There was such innocence about her, and it drew him as surely as it scared him. Perhaps they were both right to be afraid.

"Why aren't you at the party?" he finally asked.

Carly's chin lifted. "Why aren't you?"

"I thought we agreed that you would stay in the private family quarters," Holt said.

"You *assumed* we agreed."

"You didn't argue with me."

"That's because I've lived with my father long enough to know that you don't waste logic on a mind that's closed to it."

Holt's eyes narrowed and he had a sudden urge to laugh. Moments ago, she'd been as moved as he was when he'd pinned her to the wall. He'd heard her breath catch in her throat, he'd felt her body soften, her heart hammer against his. Even now her voice was a little breathless, and he could reach out and touch her pulse where it still beat quickly at her throat. Yet the light of battle was in her eyes, and she was talking about logic!

He smiled. "Normally I'm not totally immune to logic." Turning, he walked to the desk and sat on the corner. "Why don't you give it a try?"

Carly took a deep breath and let it out. That quick, engaging grin of his was almost as lethal as his touch. Desperate, she tried to focus on the problem at hand. "Okay, here it is in a nutshell. You're the expert on Carpenter Enterprises. But I know my sister. And I can offer a woman's point of view. If we work together, I know we can find out where Jenna is more quickly than if we work separately."

"Your father and I are worried about your safety. I'd be more than willing to consult with you, share information."

Carly waved a hand as she walked toward him. "You sound just like my father. And your goal is the same as his. You just want me out of the way."

Holt studied her for a moment. "Obviously, you don't intend to stay out of the way."

"You've got that right. Jenna is my sister. We can work together to find her. Or I'll find a way to work on my own."

"Explain to me how we can save time by working together."

Carly's brows shot up. "You mean it?"

Holt's smile was wry this time. "I told you I'm not immune to logic."

"All right. Your security men searched Jenna's bedroom. But I'll bet they didn't even notice the matches."

"Matches?"

"Jenna doesn't smoke. I found the matches in a box in her bottom drawer. They're from a restaurant and a dance club here in Manhattan, and I figure Jenna must have kept them as a romantic souvenir of places she's been with her lover. We can visit each place, show people a picture of Jenna. If someone remembers seeing them, we might even get a credit card receipt with a name and an address." Carly paused expectantly, but Holt's expression remained inscrutable. "You're a tough nut to crack, Cassidy. Did you find Jenna's day planner?"

"It's on the desk."

Moving around him, Carly sat in Jenna's chair and began to leaf through it. "I'll bet you that I can find something you missed." For a few moments she focused all her attention on the day planner. Using her finger, she quickly skimmed each page. When she finished, she glanced up, only to find that he'd moved to her side. His arm was resting on the chair behind her, and his face was close to hers. So close she could feel his breath against her lips.

"Sure enough, I found something."

"What is it?"

She hadn't thought it possible, but now he seemed even closer. "You have to go first." Then she met his eyes and knew she'd made a mistake. They'd reminded her of a rain forest before. But now she thought of smoke, the kind that shot up fast and hot from a bonfire. And through it she saw desire, and a flash of recklessness she hadn't noted before. A punch of fear mixed with her own desire just before his mouth covered hers.

Hard and hungry, it didn't waste time teasing or enticing. Instead, it took firm and complete possession of hers.

Nothing about his kiss surprised her. What did was her own response. She'd thought she'd braced herself. But it didn't seem to matter. She'd thought she could control everything, hold her own, but her need and the delight bubbling up in her were too much. She'd never known such intensity. Though his hand rested only along her throat, it was as if he touched every part of her. Though it was only his mouth that seduced her, it ran through her mind that he could take her right here in the office. Right on Jenna's desk. This was a man who would always reach out and take what he wanted, wherever and whenever it suited him.

Her heart was hammering so loud that she couldn't hear anything else. His mouth was so demanding that she couldn't feel anything else.

Touch me, she wanted to say. *Take me.* But it was all she could do to grip the lapels of his jacket and urge him closer.

He was very close to drowning in her, Holt realized. Whatever it was that he'd expected when he'd initiated the kiss, it hadn't been this. This fire. This inferno. Nothing had prepared him for her surrender.

He felt his mind go blank and fill with her. Her mouth was just as he'd thought it would be. Soft, pliant, warm. But the moment her lips parted and her tongue met his, her taste stunned him. Tart and sweet were the flavors on the surface. But beneath that, he tasted the rich depth of her need, and he recognized it as the perfect echo of his own. He knew in that moment that he would never forget it, never get enough of it.

Her scent wound around him too, conjuring up images of exotic flowers and steamy tropical nights. He thought of taking her on the sand with the ocean pounding on the shore. He thought of taking her on the desk. With one practiced move, he could have her beneath him. The image filled his mind, tempting him. Taunting him. It would be wild and wonderful.

And a mistake.

He gripped the edge of the desk with his free hand until his fingers ached. It was a dim shadow of the ache that was building inside him. Very slowly, Holt moved away. Her eyes were still closed. When they opened, they were still clouded with desire. And in spite of his resolve, what he wanted to do more than anything else was to kiss her again.

"Excuse me."

Holt whirled to see Susan Masterson standing in the open doorway.

"I came to check Ms. Carpenter's appointments for the next few days," she explained.

Carly wasn't sure where she found the strength, but she lifted the day planner. "That's exactly what Mr. Cassidy and I came to do." Rising, she managed to avoid Holt by moving around the opposite side of the desk. "I'm going to take it up to Jenna so she can tell me what she wants me to handle. Then I'll be in touch with you in the morning." She realized that Susan was staring at her feet. She thought of the sandals she'd dropped somewhere in the stairwell. "You're wondering what happened to my shoes. They were killing me, so I ditched them."

Susan Masterson didn't bat an eyelash at the explanation. She merely moved to a cabinet and pulled out a pair of black canvas flats. "Ms. Carpenter keeps a comfortable pair of walking shoes here so she can change when she goes out."

"Very practical of her. Thank you." There was real relief in Carly's voice as she slipped into the shoes. Then she backed quickly toward the door. Holt was there ahead of her, and taking her arm, he led her to the elevator.

It wasn't until the elevator doors closed behind them that Carly turned to face Holt. "How much do you think she saw?"

"Does it matter?"

"If she saw us kissing, that will really start the rumor mills rolling."

Holt pressed a button on the elevator.

"Aren't you worried?" Carly asked.

He shrugged. "It's really only a matter of time until everyone knows that Jenna's eloped—or been kidnapped. Talk about our kissing will have a very short lifespan."

"Right." And he was right. Carly tried to assume an indifferent attitude. After all, it was only a kiss. Obviously it hadn't affected Holt the same way it had affected her. Or perhaps he was used to being...what? *Consumed?* If that kiss had gone on much longer, she would have lost a part of herself. She risked a sidelong glance at Holt. He looked perfectly composed. As usual. And she?

Well, she still wasn't quite sure how she'd managed to talk to Susan Masterson—or walk to the elevator. There was a lesson to be learned here. She forced herself to concentrate on it. Something about her man-hunting technique was definitely working. The clothes, the makeup, whatever. At least she knew that she was capable of attracting a man like Holt. What she had to work on now was her reaction. Controlling it and us-

ing it to her advantage. She just wasn't sure she had
any note cards on that.

When the doors opened, Carly stepped automati-
cally through them, then stopped short when she realized she was in the main lobby.

"Where—?" she questioned.

"We're going someplace where we can talk and
where we won't be interrupted," Holt explained. He
wrapped his arm around her to draw her close as he
urged her through the revolving doors.

A blast of arctic wind slammed into them, and Holt
immediately shifted his body to take the brunt of it as
he hurried her to the curb. When she glimpsed an ap-
proaching cab, the thought drifted through her mind
that he might be planning to take her to his apartment.
Before she could summon up a protest, he was urging
her across the street. The next thing she knew, he was
ushering her through a door.

It was the scent she recognized first, even before she
had completely brushed the snowflakes öff her eye-
lashes. Coffee. Wide-eyed, she looked around. Booths
lined the walls of the brightly lit room. A television set
hung in one corner, but it was drowned out by the din
of conversation, the clatter of china and the steam aris-
ing from an espresso machine that sat gleaming on a
long white counter.

"A coffeehouse!" Carly beamed at Holt. "You're
wonderful!" Grabbing his arm, she led him to an
empty booth at the far corner of the room. "This is the
fourth time in one day that you've saved my life!"

"We can talk here," he said as he settled himself
across from her. "And we won't be interrupted." He
didn't add that it was also a public place, and that he'd
chosen it for his own safety as well as hers. But as he

watched her absorb the sounds and the smells with such enthusiasm, he was reminded of the fact that she'd been living far away from civilization for the past two years. And he thought of the time he'd spent traveling on freighters and his own excitement each time the ship pulled into port.

It was odd that he should think of that now. But of course, Carly Carpenter had been pulling emotions out of him from the first moment he met her. Everything from simple curiosity and amusement to raw, sexual desire.

And that presented him with a dilemma. He was very tempted to go along with her request to work with him to find her sister. Intelligence like Carly's was hard to come by. It wasn't merely her credentials. Academic degrees sometimes weren't worth the paper they were written on. But he'd seen the way her mind worked. And she'd already thought of things that he hadn't, noticed things the security people had overlooked. But he wasn't kidding himself—if they worked together, they were headed for trouble. Each moment they spent together, he was going to be tempted to take things further than the kiss they'd just shared.

She met his eyes. "This was so nice of you."

He couldn't help but be amused by the trace of surprise in her voice. "I can be nice on occasion."

"I'm sure you can. I didn't mean..."

"We also have something important to discuss. You were about to tell me what I'd overlooked in Jenna's day planner."

"Right." Carly placed it on the table. "But no cheating. You tell me first what you're going to have the security people check on. Then I'll tell you what I found."

"All right."

A waitress interrupted, but after Carly had ordered a large cappuccino and Holt a Carpenter tea, he continued. "I think it's worth checking out the meeting she has scheduled every Tuesday night at St. Anthony's. That's one night a week when no one would question her absence from the penthouse. Then there are a few lunches at restaurants. As far as I know, Jenna schedules most of her business lunches in the executive dining room."

"Good thinking." Carly nodded approvingly. "She's saved matchbooks from one of those restaurants. We definitely have to check it out. Anything else?"

Her hands were clasped tightly together. Her eyes were sparkling. She was literally bursting to tell him. Holt couldn't resist saying, "Let me have a look at the book again." He reached for it, but Carly snatched it away.

"Not on your life. I said no cheating. Now that I've let you know that there's something else, you just might find it."

"Then why do I need a partner?" Holt asked.

"To save time. If we work together, we can find Jenna faster. I'm sure of it."

"All right. What did I miss?"

"Smiley's Health Club and Gym," Carly announced as she flipped through the pages. "See. The *PT* probably stands for personal trainer, and it says *weight lifting!*"

"Jenna's been going three times a week to that place for as long as I can remember," Holt said with a frown.

Carly raised a hand. "The notations only go back six months. According to what she told me, that's when she started seeing this man. Plus, Jenna hates to work out. Ballet, yes. Maybe some aerobic dancing. Pumping iron, no."

Holt considered that for a moment, then nodded at her. "All right. I wouldn't have checked the gym. At least not until I failed to get any other leads."

"Then we're partners?" Carly asked, extending her hand. When he still hesitated, she said, "*Please*. We have to find Jenna as soon as possible."

Finally Holt capitulated, taking her hand in his. "We may both live to regret this partnership."

Carly met his eyes steadily. "If you're talking about the kiss, it's probably better if we don't do that again."

"If we work together, Carly, I can almost promise you that we'll do it again."

"Then I'll just have to learn to handle it better. Don't worry. It's my problem. I'll figure out something."

Holt couldn't prevent a grin. Reaching over, he ran a finger down her dangling earring, sending it spinning. "If you learn to handle it any better—"

"A Carpenter tea," the waitress said, setting it down. "And a cappuccino. Will there be anything else?"

"No, this will be fine," Holt murmured, leaning against the back of the booth. It was just as well the waitress had interrupted him. Carly wasn't the only one who'd have to figure out how to handle things. Holt watched her turn her full attention to the cappuccino, inhaling the steam, then taking a careful sip. When she leaned back to savor the taste, her eyes were closed, her face aglow with simple enjoyment causing his thoughts to begin wandering to situations he'd rather not think about at this moment. Taking a sip of his tea, he asked, "Why anthropology?"

Carly's eyes snapped open.

"I'm curious," he explained. "It's not the most common field of study, nor the most lucrative."

"Ah, the true corporate executive. Always concerned with the bottom line."

"It's not always money," Holt said.

Carly nodded. "True. I guess I finally chose anthropology because it lets me study so many different kinds of people, their habits, customs, the way they live. I find people fascinating."

"Why not psychology or sociology?" he asked.

Carly wrinkled her nose. "I took some courses, but I always seemed to end up studying problems and disorders. I guess I like to study positive stuff."

Holt's eyebrows rose. "And you had to go all the way to an isolated island in the Pacific in order to find something positive?"

Carly smiled. "Not exactly. I went there because it was the opportunity of a lifetime. Dr. Antolini and his wife—he was my dissertation adviser—anyway, they invited me to go with them and do some field research. I couldn't turn it down."

"Didn't you find it lonely?" Holt asked.

Carly shook her head. "The work kept me busy. But I also liked the solitude and silence and being surrounded by the sea."

Once again, Holt thought of how similar his own feelings had been during the years he'd spent working in the merchant marine. It was a time in his life that he hadn't thought about in a very long while.

A few feet away, a waitress dropped a tray, and for a moment, the air was filled with the crash of dishes followed by a round of applause from the customers.

Holt raised his teacup with a grin. "Welcome home to Manhattan."

Carly laughed and touched her cup to his. As their eyes met and held, she felt every bit as close to him as she had when she'd been in his arms. How could that possibly be? Of its own accord her gaze drifted lower to his lips. Curved in a smile, they were more tempting than ever. Perhaps because she knew exactly how they would feel pressed against hers. Warm at first, but that heat would build so quickly... Just as her thoughts began to blur, Carly managed to rein them in. Quick. She had to think of something else. Anything. She shifted her eyes to his cup and said the first thing that came to her mind. "Why tea?"

"I prefer it to coffee."

Carly leaned forward. "Yes, but how did that happen? You don't seem the type. If I were to guess your favorite drink, I'd probably say Irish whiskey straight up. Or maybe beer."

"When I was sixteen, I ran away on a tramp steamer and spent some time in the Near East. I got to know the people and learned to admire their philosophy and their drink."

Carly simply stared at him for a minute. Jenna hadn't filled her in on that part of Holt's life. Suddenly she had questions. Hundreds of them.

"You've got that look on your face again," Holt said.

"What look?"

"The same one you had while we were dancing—as if you wished you had one of your note cards handy."

Carly battled with a blush and failed. "I'm sorry. It's a horrible habit of mine. Just tell me to back off."

"Back off."

Because he said it with a smile, she laughed and took a sip of her cappuccino. Then, setting it down, she rested her arms on the table and leaned toward him. "Okay, when do we start?"

It gave her some satisfaction to see a look of wariness on his face before his eyes narrowed. She *was* going to learn to hold her own with Holt Cassidy. She was sure of it.

"Start what?" he asked.

"Our investigation. I figure it would probably be smart to visit the gym during Jenna's regular appointment time." She glanced at her watch. "And there's probably no one at St. Anthony's right now. But we could hit that restaurant and maybe the dance club."

"Slow down. The blackmailer's going to call your father at seven. I want to be there."

"Me, too. I forgot." Then she wrinkled her nose. "I just hate to wait."

Holt smiled. "I can see that."

"We can go after the call," she suggested.

Holt hesitated. "I can send one of the security people to the restaurants."

Carly reached out to grasp his hand. "No. They don't know Jenna. I want to go to all those places myself. If there's one thing I've learned the past two years, it's the value of research in the field. When you read a book or listen to a report, everything's filtered through someone else's eyes. It's different when you experience it yourself. There's bound to be something your security people will overlook. Like the matches. Please."

After a moment, Holt nodded. "You're a very persuasive woman."

She flashed him a grin as she grabbed the day planner and slid out of the booth. "Count on it."

4

BALLS SMACKED and clattered as Holt sent the five ball careening into the corner pocket.

"Damn!" Calvin muttered as he stalked to the open door that led to his office. "You keep making all that noise and we won't be able to hear the phone ring."

"Sorry," Holt replied, then silently slipped the next three balls into three different pockets.

Calvin swore again and paced back to the table. "When are they going to call?"

"Just as soon as they think they've got you ready to agree to anything," Holt replied calmly as he cleared another ball.

"Humph!" Calvin clamped his teeth down on an unlit cigar.

Carly hid a smile. Holt had suggested a game of pool to pass the time while they waited for the blackmailer's call. And for almost two hours it had distracted them, just as he'd intended it to do. Not that she'd been invited to play. She hadn't even been aware that her father had a pool table in the library that opened off his office.

Obviously, Calvin believed pool was a man's game. The room itself was dramatically masculine with its leather furniture and wine-colored drapes. But nine ball was another matter entirely. Carly was sure a woman could master it as easily as a man.

Logically, it seemed pretty simple. It had taken her less than two games to jot down the rules on one of her note cards. The tricky part was visualizing the proper geometric patterns and figuring the velocity. Then there was manual dexterity to think about. Her eyes returned to Holt's hands. Somehow, it didn't surprise her at all that he was very good at it.

A few moments ago, he'd broken the balls, and then he'd begun to systematically clear the table. But occasionally there was a recklessness to his play that broke the pattern.

It was the recklessness that intrigued Carly. It reminded her of the flash she'd seen in his eyes just before he'd kissed her. She'd been thinking about that kiss a lot, but so far she hadn't quite decided how she was going to handle the next one. Of course, the safest strategy would be to make sure there wasn't a next time. But from what she knew of Holt, she wasn't sure the choice would be entirely up to her.

It was a risky and complicated shot he was setting up now. Without thinking, she moved closer to the table. Leaning forward, Holt banked a ball off the side, sending it at a clean angle into two other balls. One slipped into a center pocket, the other disappeared into the corner.

"Damn!" Calvin muttered. "How the hell did you do that?"

The phone in the office rang before Holt could answer. Turning, he walked over to Calvin's desk and punched the button to turn on the speaker.

A mechanically distorted voice filled the room. "Tit for tat. Load the formula and all the research results on computer disks. Tomorrow I'll call back at seven with an E-mail address."

"We need more time," Holt said firmly. "Not all of the research is available in-house. Thursday is the soonest I can promise it. And we want to talk to Jenna."

There was a pause. Then another voice filled the room.

"Daddy...do what...they say."

Calvin moved forward. "Jenna, honey, are you all right? Have they hurt you?"

It was the mechanical voice that responded. "Tomorrow at seven."

"It can't be done," Holt replied. "We need until Thursday to gather everything together."

Calvin opened his mouth. Holt raised a hand to signal silence, and Carly took her father's hand in hers. Then they waited, their eyes fastened on the phone. Five seconds stretched into ten, then fifteen.

"Wednesday at seven. If you want to see Jenna again."

"Don't you touch my daughter," Calvin roared as he leaned toward the phone. The only reply was a dial tone.

Holt turned off the speaker. "The caller ID box says out of area." Picking up the receiver, he punched in a phone number. "Did you get anything?" Then he turned to Calvin and Carly. "The call wasn't long enough to trace."

Calvin met Holt's eyes squarely. "We've only got until Wednesday."

"We'll have to make every moment count," Holt said as he settled himself into a chair. "First thing tomorrow, Carly and I are going to check out some places she found on Jenna's day planner."

"I thought we decided Carly would be safer if she stayed here in the penthouse," Calvin said.

Holt shrugged. "I'll be with her. She's a woman and she knows Jenna. There could be something she'll see that you or I might miss."

Eyes narrowed, Calvin looked at his daughter and then back at Holt. "I'll come with you."

Holt shook his head. "You need to be here. It's important that everything seems as normal as possible. And you're the best person to keep an eye on Chadwick, Gallagher and Miller. It might not hurt to put a little pressure on them, let them know they're being watched."

"Jenna sounded funny," Carly said suddenly.

Both men turned to her.

"It was *her* voice," Calvin said.

"What sounded funny?" Holt asked.

Carly frowned as she tried to put her finger on exactly what it was that she'd heard. "Something about her inflection. She didn't sound frightened. And the space between words..."

"They could have used recordings of her voice, then spliced the words together," Holt said. "We didn't get to talk to her. We just listened."

"What are you saying?" Calvin demanded.

"The blackmailer might not really have her," Carly replied. "She might not be kidnapped. But that means she could be—" She stopped short as a more frightening possibility struck her, and she raised terrified eyes to Holt's.

"Not necessarily. We can't be sure of anything except that the tape of Jenna's voice might have been doctored. You could still be right that she's off somewhere enjoying her honeymoon. It won't do us any good to jump to rash conclusions. What we should concentrate on is the blackmailer." Switching his attention to Calvin, Holt continued in the same calm voice. "Whoever this person is, he's smart. He anticipated that we would want to speak to Jenna, and he was prepared. Also, an E-mail address will most likely be impossible to trace."

Carly settled herself on the couch while the two men reviewed strategy for the next fifteen minutes. Calvin pulled a bottle of brandy out of his bottom drawer, and by the time Holt rose to leave, she could see that most of the tension had drained from her father's face.

After giving Calvin a quick kiss good-night, she followed Holt out into the hall. He was waiting by the elevator, his face in the shadows, but she could see from his stance that he was tired. It occurred to her again how alone he looked.

Moving toward him, she said, "Thank you. I appreciate the way that you handled my father—I mean, about our working together—and it was nice of you to stay until he was more relaxed about the phone call."

Holt's lips curved. "That's the second time today you've accused me of being nice."

"Yes," she said, moving closer.

He reached up to run a finger over her earring and send it spinning. "Don't be fooled," he warned. "I'm not a nice man."

For a moment, neither of them spoke. Neither of them moved. Carly thought she knew what would happen if she stepped forward. She could see it in his eyes. It was the same struggle that was going on inside of her. If she just reached out to touch him, she could end it. And she could know again what it was like to have his mouth pressed against hers, to feel the excitement and the bright explosion of pleasure. To lose herself in it and forget the fear that had settled cold and hard in her stomach from the moment she'd heard Jenna's voice on the speaker phone. She felt the pull, stronger than ever, to take that step.

Just then, the elevator doors opened, and Holt stepped through them. "I'll grab a taxi, and I'll meet you outside tomorrow at nine."

Carly stared at him as the doors slid shut. He hadn't touched her. He'd just jiggled her earring. And yet it had been enough to rekindle all the desire she'd felt earlier. Long after the elevator had ceased humming, Carly stood in the darkened hallway, wondering what she had gotten herself into.

"I NEED A COAT!" Carly said as she searched frantically through Jenna's closet.

"Mmmroow" was Priscilla's sleepy comment from her throne at the foot of the bed.

"This should do it," she said as she grabbed the longest garment she could find. It wasn't just the frosty Manhattan weather she was thinking of. Nor the wind that had been whistling at the windows all night. No, she had quite a different reason for choosing maximum coverage. Once more she turned to look at her reflection in the full-length mirror, and once more she saw a stranger.

Jenna's workout clothes were probably the height of fashion. But the turquoise spandex top left almost as much skin showing as her bra did, and the pants, while they covered her legs all the way to her ankles, left absolutely nothing to the imagination. In fact, the young ladies who danced half-naked in the moonlight on Manilai would seem overdressed compared to this.

For just a moment, Carly hesitated. It was one thing to come up with a plan. Carrying it out was another matter. Last night after Holt had left, it had seemed so simple. After all, she was perfectly capable of doing two things at once. But in the light of day, everything suddenly seemed terribly complicated.

There had to be a way to make it all work. Her first priority was to find out where Jenna had gone. But that didn't mean that she couldn't continue her campaign to attract Holt Cassidy at the same time. Did it?

Besides, what choice did she have? The blackmailer was calling back tomorrow night, and the wedding was scheduled two days after that. Lifting her chin, Carly faced herself squarely in the mirror. She'd faced tough deadlines before and met them.

That was why she'd stayed up late into the night reviewing her research. The young women on Manilai married much earlier than women in the States, and on the surface, they seemed to be much more limited in choice. But from what she'd been able to observe, they managed to do a lot of maneuvering within the choices given them. While it was true they used makeup, jewelry and clothes, or the lack of them, to get a man's attention, they also employed other techniques. Proximity was one.

There was one case study in particular that fit this situation and she'd searched through her boxes for hours looking for her cards. In her notes she'd referred to the young woman as Lania. The young man Lania "chose" was Lu, one of the finest fishermen in the village. But Lania wasn't the only woman who favored Lu. The difference was that she eventually married him. And one of the most striking yet subtle things she'd done was to simply make sure she got in his way as often as possible. She'd managed to cross his path each morning as he went to his boat and each evening when he came home.

The other thing Lania had done was to play a waiting game. Lania didn't throw herself at Lu the same way that the other women did. And occasionally she would show an interest in other men, always while Lu was watching.

Slipping into the coat, Carly walked to the dresser, where she'd left her note card describing Lania's techniques. Frowning, she picked it up and turned toward the foot of the bed, where Priscilla was regarding her through slitted eyes.

"These suggestions looked better in the middle of the night." With a sigh, she sat down beside the cat. "Number one, plan for proximity—keep close. That's easy. I'm going to be with him most of the day checking out Jenna's suspicious appointments. Number two, keep your distance. Not so easy. Whenever I'm close to him..." She turned to face the cat. "I don't fully understand it. I've never felt this way before. But I want to touch him. I want him to touch me."

Priscilla blinked sleepily at her.

"Pay attention. I need some advice here."

Priscilla merely blinked again.

"All right. I know that I have to keep him at arm's length if I want my brain to function properly. And I need to be able to think straight if I'm going to find out anything about Jenna. So I'll find a way to keep my distance." Carly glanced back down at her notes. "Number three, show an interest in other men. That's a great idea, but practically speaking, I've never flirted with anybody in my life."

"Mmmrow," Priscilla said as she settled her head on her paws and closed her eyes.

"Bragger!" Carly stuck her tongue out at the cat before she glanced back at her notes. There wasn't a doubt in her mind that the spandex outfit would attract some attention. If she could just carry it off... Not that she intended to use it on the priest at St. Anthony's. That was why she needed a coat at least until she got to Smiley's gym. Tucking the note card into her pocket, she rose and moved to the mirror for one last inspection. The coat had a wide fake-fur collar and fell nearly to her ankles. She certainly looked decent. She also looked like an Eskimo.

Well, until they got to the gym, she'd have to rely on the earrings to attract Holt. Moving her head, she set the dangling gold balls dancing. The women on Manilai spent hours creating necklaces and bracelets out of shells and pretty stones. But Holt seemed to like earrings. She was wearing the same ones she'd worn yesterday, the ones he'd touched in the coffee shop and then again before he'd left last night. He'd run his finger down one, and it had been enough to make her wonder. And want.

With a frown she reined in her wandering thoughts. *Keep your distance, Carly,* she reminded herself. *And get going.*

A quick glance at her watch told her she had fifteen minutes to deal with Susan Masterson if she wanted to meet Holt outside by nine o'clock. Deadlines. Fastening the buttons on the coat, she raced out of the room.

THE STEEL GRAY CLOUDS threatening overhead were a perfect match for Holt's mood as he watched the glass doors to the Carpenter Building. Nine-twenty and there was still no sign of Carly. He was ready to release the cab he was holding and go in search of her when she burst through the doors, then came to a skidding halt at the curb. The second she spotted him standing across the street, she waved and sent him a beaming smile.

Stick to her like glue! That was the terse command Calvin had given him in his office earlier. He wondered if the older man had any idea how tempted he was to do just that. Whatever Calvin knew or sensed about his feelings for Carly, the wily old fox sure knew how to play a waiting game. Not once had he asked Holt whether or not he intended to accept Carly's proposal. No, Calvin wouldn't bring it up until Holt did.

Stick to her like glue. The image held far too much appeal. And that was a problem. It had taken a long time for him to fall asleep last night. And for most of the night, he'd been trying to figure out what to do about Carly Carpenter. The rest of the night, he'd been caught up in the memory of the kiss they'd shared in Jenna's office.

Even now, he had an urge to repeat the experience. To see if that same intense explosion of feeling would happen again. But to give in to the urge would be dangerous. Self-control was a habit he'd built up carefully over the years, yet it threatened to shatter whenever he was near Carly.

His eyes narrowed as he watched her teeter on the curb in her impatience to cross the street. In the long coat with its fake-fur collar, she looked as if she might actually belong in one of those primitive tribes she studied. All too easily, an image slipped into his mind of Carly, standing in a cave, lit only by firelight. Even more easily, he could picture what it might be like to slip her out of that coat and watch the movement of that flickering, soft light on her skin. Then he would trace that movement with his hands and mold slowly, very slowly, every inch...

A sharp, impatient blast of a horn brought him back to the present. Carly was smiling and waving an irate driver along while she halted for a second in the middle of the street, then scooted behind one car and dashed in front of another. Holt's lips curved as he watched her. She crossed the street the way she did everything, it seemed. In a rush. He, on the other hand, preferred to take his time, weigh his options.

And at some point in the middle of the night, he'd decided that making love to Carly wasn't one of them. There were too many things on his plate right now. Finding Jenna had to be his first priority. So he couldn't afford to touch her again. Not until they got Jenna back safely.

"Sorry I'm late," she said as she skidded to a stop in front of him. "My meeting with Susan took a little longer than I expected. Then I ran into Mark and Tom and Danny at the elevator. Of course, they wanted to know how Jenna was, and then I had to explain where I was going..." She let the sentence trail off as Holt opened the back door of the taxi and reached in for a paper tray.

"Coffee?" She breathed the word like a prayer. At his nod, she reached for the cup he offered. "And you claim you're not a nice man."

"I'm a practical man," Holt said as he gestured her into the cab. "We have work to do, and I don't want you going into withdrawal."

Leaning forward, Carly gave the taxi driver the address for St. Anthony's, then held tight to her coffee as the cab shot out into the traffic. "There was a phone number for St. Anthony's rectory in Jenna's Rolodex, along with a Father Finelli's name. I called ahead, and he's expecting us."

Holt turned to study her. "I see. I suppose you also have a plan?"

She nodded and carefully took a sip of her coffee. "I thought it might be best if I went in alone—"

"Forget it, Carly. I promised your father I wouldn't let you out of my sight."

She shot him a quick grin. "It was worth a shot. And I might have been able to pull it off better on my own. But the second part of the plan's the important part. If Jenna's been seeing this priest every Tuesday for the past six months, she might have confided in him. But he won't part with that information easily. So I think we ought to tell Father Finelli the truth."

"It's too risky," Holt said.

"But he's a priest," Carly argued. "We could make him promise to keep the information confidential. And if we're absolutely honest with him and explain that Jenna might be in danger, he might be persuaded to share something—anything—that Jenna might have told him in confidence."

"You're too trusting, Carly. We can't take a chance on any of this being leaked to the press, for Jenna's sake as well as the company's. Even if we take the best-case scenario, your theory that someone is taking advantage of Jenna's elopement to blackmail Carpenter Enterprises, it might *seem* that Jenna isn't in any real danger. But we don't know what that person might do if he thinks we aren't taking the blackmail threat seriously."

Frowning, Carly considered Holt's argument as the taxi lurched into a sudden left turn. The problem was it was logical. Sometimes she hated logic. She drained the contents of her cup before she said, "All right. We'll do it your way. But I still think I'm right."

She'd barely finished the sentence when the cab stopped in front of a very old church. Though the bricks had faded to pink and the paint on the trim was peeling, it still had a kind of quiet beauty. As did the house that adjoined it. The rectory, Carly decided as she waited for Holt to pay the driver. The rest of the block was filled with tenement buildings, the same approximate age as the church.

For the first time, Carly began to wonder what it was that had drawn her sister out of her sheltered uptown apartment into this obviously less affluent neighborhood.

"Welcome to SoHo," Holt said as he joined her. "I told the cab to wait for us."

Nodding, she let him lead the way up the rectory steps. The man who answered their ring didn't fit Carly's image of a priest at all. A few inches under six feet, with the lean, wiry build of a lightweight boxer, the young man looked as if he'd be more at home in a gym than a rectory. But he was wearing a collar, and his smile was warm and welcoming.

"Father Finelli, I'm Carly Carpenter, Jenna's sister, and this is Holt Cassidy, her fiancé."

The priest's smile faded slightly as he glanced quickly from Carly to Holt. He hesitated a moment before he accepted Holt's outstretched hand, then he stepped back into the foyer. "Come in. It's nice to meet Jenna's family. She's done a lot for this parish." Turning, he led them down a narrow hallway to a large room that smelled of the books that lined the room from floor to ceiling. Carly also smelled coffee. A pot and three mugs sat on the edge of a large desk piled high with papers and files.

After gesturing them into two chairs, Father Finelli sat on the edge of the desk. "How can I help you?" he asked.

"We've come to offer our help to you, Father," Holt explained. "Jenna has come down with the flu, and Carly has promised her that she'll substitute for her at all of her engagements before the wedding on Friday."

The priest said nothing, merely shifting his somewhat puzzled gaze from Holt to Carly.

"She's under medication from the doctor," Carly said. "All we have to go by is her day planner, and she has St. Anthony's written in tonight at seven. If you'll just tell me what I have to do..."

"There's not a thing to do," Father Finelli said. "Jenna has set up the mentoring program so that it runs itself. Each week, she's arranged for women in different professions to come and speak to our girls." He consulted a calendar on his desk. "Tonight it's Dr. Roberta Wrenfield, a research biologist from Sloan Kettering Memorial, and next week it's Margaret Lazenby, a reporter with WKNY-TV."

"You weren't expecting Jenna to be here, then?" Holt asked.

"No, she's never here," Father Finelli replied. "Well, that is except for one time in October when one of the women canceled at the last minute. But I don't want to downplay her contribution. We wouldn't have the program without her. She contacts the speakers and does all the administrative work." Stepping away from the desk, he gave them an apologetic smile. "I'm sorry you came all this way for nothing."

Rising, Holt started for the door, but Carly remained

seated. "Do you mind my asking how Jenna got involved in this program, Father? She's not a member of your parish, is she?"

"Well, no." He started to sit back down on the edge of his desk, then seemed to think better of it. "It was quite a coincidence. I won a three-month trial membership at her gym, Smiley's." He folded his hands, then dropped them to his sides. "We got to talking, and the next thing I knew, she offered to set up this program. It was a lucky day for St. Anthony's." Turning, he walked toward Holt, who was waiting at the door.

"One more thing, Father Finelli," Carly said. "Did Jenna come here alone that night in October?"

Slowly, the priest faced her. "No. No, she didn't."

"Did she come with a man?" Carly asked as she rose and walked toward him.

Father Finelli shifted his gaze to Holt, then back to Carly. "I'm sorry, but I just don't feel...I think you should ask your sister."

Carly reached out to him and took his hand. "Please, I can't tell you why, but it's very important that we find out."

The priest let out the breath he was holding. "Yes, she came with a man."

"Do you know who he was? Had you ever seen him before?" Carly asked.

"His name was Lance. That's all I knew him by. We went by first names at the gym."

"He was with Jenna at the gym?" Holt asked.

"We were all there together. We had the same personal trainer. Lance introduced me to Jenna."

"Thank you, Father." Carly squeezed his hand before she released it. "You've been a big help. And you mustn't think for a minute that you've betrayed Jenna. You haven't."

Carly managed to keep quiet until they reached the cab. Then she couldn't contain herself. "Well, what do you think?"

Holt turned to study her for a moment. Her eyes were lit with excitement. It seemed to radiate from her in much the same way that energy radiated from the sun. A sudden gust of wind whipped at them, carrying a spray of snow and tiny ice pellets. Reaching for the lapels of her coat, he tugged them together and fastened the top button. Then he brushed his fingers over the collar to smooth the fur away from her face. "I'm impressed, partner."

For a second, Carly didn't speak. She wasn't sure she could. Was it the compliment or his hand fiddling with her coat that had her hearing her own heartbeat? Before she could summon up even one word, Holt continued, "How did you know he was hiding something?"

A question, she thought with relief. She would focus on that. "Body language."

Holt frowned. "I thought he was just nervous and a little embarrassed because we'd made a trip down here for nothing."

Carly managed a smile. "I have more experience with it than you do. Any anthropologist who does research in the field has to become an expert on it. Because of language barriers, we often have to rely on body language alone. I noticed that Father Finelli was surprised the moment I introduced you as Jenna's fiancé, and he was very anxious to get rid of us."

"I assumed he was just busy. All those files on his desk."

"He'd made a pot of coffee, but he didn't offer us any."

Holt smiled at her. "That's the caffeine addict, not the anthropologist, talking."

Carly shrugged. "Could be. But I wouldn't have had to tap into my expertise at all if we'd gone with my first plan. Why don't you admit that I was right? We could have told him the truth."

Holt's smile faded. "No, I won't admit that. You're too trusting, Carly. Hasn't anyone ever betrayed you?"

"No...well, maybe once." She shifted her gaze quickly to the taxi and opened the door.

Holt settled himself beside her in the cab and pulled the door shut. She was staring out the window, her hands clasped tightly together in her lap.

"Who?" he asked.

"The truth is, I'm not really sure..."

"Who?" Holt asked again.

"It's a long story," Carly said.

"It's going to be a long ride to the gym," Holt replied as he leaned forward to give the driver the address. Then he turned back to Carly. "Even longer if I have to tell the driver to take us on a tour of Central Park on our way there."

When she met his eyes, she could see the determination in them. "All right. But you're going to be bored to death. When I was in graduate school, I thought I was in love with one of my professors. If I'd had a little more experience or been a little more savvy...but I wasn't. I was so focused on my studies that I wasn't privy to most of the campus gossip." With a sigh, she raised her hands and dropped them. "See? I'm still trying to make excuses. I had an affair with this man without ever bothering to find out that he was married."

Holt's eyes narrowed. It was the second time in less than twenty-four hours that she'd made him feel jealous. This time the sensation was ripe and hot and he wanted to strangle someone. "*He* knew he was married. He betrayed you *and* his wife. Why are you trying to take the blame?"

She met his eyes squarely. "I shouldn't have been so gullible."

"You were young and innocent, and he should be shot."

His eyes weren't hooded now. For a moment her voice dried up and her stomach muscles tightened. This was the ruthlessness she'd sensed in him from the very beginning. The carefully leashed power of the predator. Primitive, raw, basic. In another time, another society, he would have killed for her.

Instead of shocking her, the thought thrilled her to the bone. Later, she would tell herself that she should have drawn away. Instead, she leaned forward, covered one of his hands with hers and laid the other along his cheek. To calm? To provoke? She wasn't sure. Nothing she'd ever read or observed had prepared her for what she was feeling. She wasn't even sure she could summarize it on a note card. The only thing she was certain of was the instant change she saw in his eyes from anger to desire. And the echoing response she felt deep within her.

He didn't dare touch her, Holt told himself. If he did, he might not be able to stop. The realization surprised him, as did the effort he had to exert to keep his own hands still while hers were on him. Did she have any idea what she was doing to him? he wondered. What those small, elegant hands were doing? They rested on his cheek and his hand, but it was enough to make him ache.

He thought he'd experienced desire before, in all its varieties. But this was different. Desire was simple. What he was feeling for Carly was complicated, confusing and darned near impossible to control.

"Thank you," she said, "for wanting to kill him. I did myself."

"You what?"

His shocked look had her smiling. "I *wanted* to kill him. But I didn't. Have you ever killed anyone?"

His eyes darkened. "Back off, Carly."

"Sorry. I suppose that was rude."

"Abominably."

"I just thought since I bared my soul to you, you might be willing to reciprocate."

"So you can record it on one of your note cards? I think not. We're here," Holt said as the cab jerked to the curb. "It's right across the street."

"Already? We haven't even discussed strategy."

"That's easy," Holt replied with a grin. "Isn't this what you call field research? You can follow me around and take notes."

In a pig's eye, Carly thought as she watched him lean forward to pay the cab driver. In fact, she wasn't even going to wait to follow him into the gym. Opening her door, she stepped quickly out into the street. The gym's entrance was on a narrow one-way road lined on either side by parked and even a few double-parked cars. She'd taken two steps before she caught the sudden blur of movement out of the corner of her eye.

A car? Even as the image filled her mind, it was followed by a flash of fear so bright it almost blinded her.

And then she couldn't think at all. Not while the car was bearing down on her. There was no time to calculate the distance to the opposite curb. No time to decide. It was pure instinct combined with momentum that thrust her forward.

But the curb seemed so far away. The roar of the engine so close. Her feet weren't moving fast enough. She wasn't going to make it. The thought flashed into her mind at the same instant that the spurt of panic shot into her throat. And then her hands slammed into the window of a parked car. Even as she flattened herself against it, she felt the rush of wind, and then the quick, hard tug at her coat as the car brushed against it. Desperately, she clung to the car, her fingers searching for a grip as she felt herself falling.

5

"CARLY!" Racing toward her, Holt didn't recognize his own voice. It sounded raw and thin. And his hands, as he reached for her, shook. Lifting her from her knees, he dragged her against him and held tight. Over her head, he saw the dark blue car race through the red light at the corner. The license plate was covered with slush.

"Are you all right?" He could feel her nod against his shoulder, but she didn't pull away. And he didn't release her.

He was still replaying every minute of what had just happened in his mind. It was the noise of the engine that had first alerted him. And then he'd seen her in the middle of the street with the car bearing down on her. That was when the terror had gripped him, turning his body to ice. The damn taxi had been between them, slowing him down as he raced around it. And then he couldn't reach her. Not without stepping into the path of the racing car himself. The panic had risen up again as he saw the car graze her and pull at her coat. If it had caught on the material, dragged her along...

Holt forced himself to swallow the hard lump of terror in his throat as he drew Carly even closer. Slowly, he moved his hand up her back over the fur collar to rest on the nape of her neck. Even through the thickness of her coat, he could feel how slender she was, how fragile. Gently he began to knead the muscles, and when she sighed, he felt his own fear finally begin to flow out of him like water. It was only moments ago in the car that he'd imagined holding her like this, touching her. Yet he hadn't once imagined it would feel like this. So natural. So right.

The realization stunned him. A part of him wanted to release her. But another part of him kept his hands right where they were. "You're sure you're not hurt?" he asked.

Carly leaned back, just far enough to meet his eyes. As usual, they told her nothing about what he was thinking. She wasn't sure what she was thinking herself. Only seconds ago, she'd been so terrified. And now she felt fine. The fear had slipped away the moment he'd taken her into his arms.

She didn't understand it. There were a lot of things she'd imagined she'd find in Holt Cassidy's arms. And she'd imagined quite a bit. But she hadn't expected to find...what? Comfort? Peace? She simply couldn't figure it out. But she would.

Summoning up a smile, she stepped away. "I'm fine. But I'm beginning to have real reservations about living in Manhattan. This is the third time since I've come home that I've been in danger of bodily injury." Turning, she began to brush away some of the slush on her coat.

Holt grabbed her arm. "Third time?"

"Remember the backpack snatcher in front of your apartment. And then there was a rude person at the party yesterday who pushed me down the stairs just before I discovered you in Jenna's office."

Holt's grip on her arm tightened. "Someone pushed you down the stairs? Explain."

Too late, Carly remembered that she hadn't intended to tell him about the incident, and by the time she finished, she could see he was angry.

"Why didn't you mention this before?"

"Because I didn't want to be put under house arrest. Besides, it isn't necessarily connected to this or to the young thug at your apartment building."

"*You* just connected the three incidents," Holt pointed out.

"I was trying to make a joke about the dangers of living in Manhattan."

"It isn't funny. The young man who tried to take your pack in front of my apartment building yesterday had a car waiting for him around the corner. Otherwise, I would have caught him."

Carly tried to ignore the knot of fear that was forming in her stomach. "What are you saying?"

"What if he was after you instead of your backpack?"

Realizing that her mouth was open, Carly shut it. Her mind was racing, trying to keep up with Holt's. "And you think that car deliberately tried to—"

"What I think is that I should have stuck to my original plan to keep you safe at the Carpenter Building." Holt's tone was grim as he urged her up on the curb.

"Yeah, well, I wasn't safe in that stairwell."

At the door to the gym, Holt turned to face her squarely. "Believe me, that's the only reason I'm not taking you back there right now. I figure you're safer here with me. But from now on, we're going to stick to each other like glue. Understood?"

Carly nodded. She understood perfectly. But what she understood and what she intended to do were two different things.

A HALF HOUR LATER, Carly was sure she was going to die of boredom unless heat prostration got her first. And Holt wasn't doing one thing to protect her from it. He wasn't sticking to her like glue, either! In fact, after he'd ordered her a Celery-Asparagus Surprise at the health bar, he'd abandoned her completely for one of the club's fitness consultants, a pert little number barely out of her teens, with a spray of hair spouting out of the top of her head. Carly hadn't quite decided whether it reminded her more of a mushroom-shaped cloud or the blowhole of a whale in full operation. But Holt certainly seemed fascinated with it.

They were cozily seated, knee to knee, three stools down from hers at the health bar. She had a perfect view of them in the wall-to-ceiling mirror behind the bar. The bubbly little consultant giggled suddenly at something Holt said and ran a hand down his arm. When Holt leaned closer to whisper something in the young woman's ear, something very sharp twisted in Carly's stomach. They might be discussing a lifetime gold membership in the club, but their bodies were having quite a different conversation, one that spoke blatantly of incentives and added benefits.

And she was *not* jealous. It was a little litany that she'd repeated to herself several times. The fact that her complexion in the mirror matched the pale green liquid in the drink that Holt had ordered for her was due entirely to the artificial lighting. But the moment she heard Holt's quick and easy burst of laughter, she wanted nothing more than to walk over, grab the woman by her mushroom-shaped head and drag her to the floor.

The only thing that kept her on her stool was that she knew Holt was merely trying to get information about

Jenna. Any minute now, he was going to convince Ms. Blowhole to let him see the membership list so that he could discover if this was the health club his friend Lance belonged to.

Carly once more faced her reflection in the mirror. The truth was, she was feeling sorry for herself because Holt was angry with her. She could tell herself that there was no logical reason for his anger, but she knew very well that emotions rarely sprang from logic. And the proof of Holt's anger was sitting right in front of her. Why else would he have ordered her the Celery-Asparagus Surprise? It had all the flavor of fizzy cat litter.

Out of the corner of her eye, she saw peppy health club consultant maneuver her stool so that her thigh was plastered against Holt's. Something inside of Carly snapped. There was absolutely no reason for her to be sitting here, melting in her coat, just because Holt was mad at her.

So what if he'd ordered her to *stay put*. The man had obviously been a CEO for so long that he'd forgotten what a true partnership was.

Slipping her hand into her pocket, she fingered the note card. She had a perfectly good plan, and it was about time she carried it out.

Unbuttoning the top three buttons of her coat, she let it slip from her shoulders. She didn't know much about flirting, but after thirty minutes of watching little Ms. Blowhole, she must have picked up something. Fixing her gaze on the young bar attendant, she aimed a brilliant smile at him.

He grabbed a pitcher of green liquid and hurried forward. "Refill, miss?"

Carly clamped her hand over the top of her glass just

in time. "No." Then she leaned toward him. "I was wondering if you could help me out. A good friend of mine had a trial membership in this club a few months back. A Father Finelli?"

"Mike?" The young man smiled. "Sure. His favorite drink is Carrot Frappé. Would you like to try it?"

Carly managed to control a shudder. "No thanks. What I'd really like to know is who his personal trainer is." She widened her smile and tried blinking her eyes. "He raved about him."

"Bartender, I'd like to settle up."

It was Holt who'd spoken, and as the young attendant hurried to the cash register, Carly's eyes locked with his in the mirror.

Stay put. The message couldn't have been more clear if he'd shouted it, Carly thought. Folding her hands in front of her, she waited until he'd paid his bill and followed Ms. Blowhole into a glassed-in office behind the registration desk.

The entrance level of Smiley's Health Club and Gym was a circular balcony with several glassed-in rooms opening off it. Besides the offices, there was a large room where a step class was being conducted and another that contained treadmills, stationary bikes and several other trendy aerobic machines. The health bar alone was unenclosed, and it offered a view of the lower level that looked to be a very serious gym with state-of-the-art equipment. Carly had yet to see a woman working out down there.

The moment the bar attendant had finished serving a customer, Carly lowered her coat even further and sent him another smile. He winked at her as he hurried over. This flirting business wasn't so difficult after all, she thought.

"You were saying?" he asked as he leaned against the counter.

"Father Finelli's trainer," she prompted. "He told me I should ask for him."

"That'd be Sal Riccio," the young man said. Leaning a little further over the counter, he pointed through the spokes in the railing to a solidly built man with a Yankee baseball cap on his head. He was engaged in getting the better of a punching bag on the lower level. "Sal doesn't very often work with women, though. In fact, there's only one that I know of. He manages to discourage most of them from even using the gym level." He put his hand over Carly's. "But I'd be happy to work with you myself. I'm only part-time here at the bar."

"Thanks," Carly said, and eased her hand from beneath his, then gave it a pat. "But I have to try my luck with Sal first. The woman he's working with is my sister. I'm sure she'll give me a recommendation."

Slipping out of the coat, she draped it over a chair, then turned to give the bar attendant a wave before she hurried toward the circular staircase. This flirting business was a lot easier than it looked, she thought again. And she was better at it than she'd imagined she'd be. Her foot was on the top step when she felt the prickle of alarm at the back of her neck.

Turning, she saw Holt staring at her through the glass-walled office. The expression on his face was not happy. In fact, it was furious. She could almost feel the heat of his gaze on her skin. But the pretty little consultant was hovering close, her mushroom-shaped hairdo tickling against his ear.

Tit for tat! Carly beamed a smile at him before she raced down the stairs. Once she reached the bottom, she knew she'd entered a man's world. The air was liberally laced with testosterone, the smell of sweat and the sound of grunts. A man struggling to lift a bar loaded with weights was swearing low and fluently.

As she made her way across the floor, skirting a few benches, she tried to picture the way Lania would walk across the sand whenever Lu was watching. It was a slow, fluid movement, much slower than she was used to walking. But it wasn't so hard, she thought, and prayed that she didn't dislocate something. Then she grinned in delight when a man pulling weights up the wall with two ropes stopped, stared and let the weights drop to the floor.

When she reached Sal Riccio, she sat down on an unoccupied weight bench and watched. His back was to her, and it was slick with sweat. He was built like a rock. It was only as he turned and she caught a glimpse of his profile that she saw he was older, perhaps in his late forties. The only clues were the laugh lines near his eyes and the flecks of gray in the hair that crept out from beneath a Yankees cap.

The punching bag was long, almost as tall as she was, and thick. She judged it to weigh just under two hundred pounds. And Sal Riccio was giving it a beating. He had his fists raised high; one was always protecting his chin while the other moved like lightning into the bag. But it was his feet that fascinated her most. Though the pattern was seemingly erratic, there was a steady rhythm to their movement, almost like a dance. Carly wished with longing for a note card, then with a brief glance around the room remembered where she was. Her memory would have to do, she thought, turning back to concentrate on Sal.

Carly had no idea how long she'd been watching

him when he finally quit and reached for a towel. Rising from the bench, she said, "Mr. Riccio."

He whirled on her with a frown. "What—"

She smiled at him and extended her hand. "I'm Carly Carpenter. You work with my sister, Jenna. She's feeling under the weather today—"

"Told me she'd be out of town. I don't expect her back for two weeks."

Carly kept her smile firmly in place. "She didn't want many people to know about the trip. I wasn't sure whom she'd told."

Sal Riccio's eyes narrowed as he studied her up and down. "You look a little like her." Then he gripped her hand. "What can I do for you?"

"Can you teach me how to box?"

Sal stared at her for a moment, then burst into a hearty laugh. "You're serious?"

"Absolutely."

"Then you're not a bit like your sister. She just likes to tone her muscles." Lifting her arm, he said, "Show me your biceps."

When she did, he tested it, then said. "You want to box, you're gonna have to build that up." His gaze wandered down her. "Those legs look good. You need strong legs for boxing."

"I knew it!" Carly said as she let him lead her toward his gym bag. "I was watching your feet. The footwork is just as important as the punching, isn't it?"

"More important," Sal Riccio assured her as he pulled out a roll of gauze. "But we'll start with your fists." After wrapping her knuckles in several layers of the gauze, he urged her toward the punching bag, then stood behind her and gripped her wrists. "Rule number one, always protect your chin." Together they pounded her right fist into the bag.

HOLT TIGHTENED HIS GRIP on the balcony railing and bit back a snarl. No wonder Calvin had warned him to stick to Carly like glue. She was like quicksilver. There was no telling what she'd do next. And she was in danger. Didn't she realize that? He could still picture the way that car had brushed against her, almost dragging her— The sound of Carly's laughter brought him back to the present.

In one more minute, he was going to go down to the gym level and physically separate her from the man who had wrapped himself around her to demonstrate the basics of a left jab. Only one thing was delaying him. The bartender had confirmed that the man in the Yankees cap was the trainer Father Finelli had mentioned. The fitness consultant had located membership records for three Lances. They needed a last name.

In thirty seconds, he was going to get in a little punching practice himself. Not on the bag, but on the trainer who was taking the word *personal* just a little too literally.

Not that he could blame the guy. The outfit Carly was wearing had Touch Me written all over it. He'd noticed her legs were long before, but in blue spandex, they were nothing short of a miracle. Right now that miracle was on very public display.

The moment the trainer stepped back from her, she executed a fancy little step and sent a solid one-two punch into the bag. As Holt watched it sway under the impact, he realized that she was good. Her footwork had a natural rhythm, and each jab she threw was hitting home. She might have gone down there with the idea of pumping Jenna's personal trainer for information, but she'd thrown herself one hundred percent into the boxing lesson. Just as she'd thrown herself into the task of investigating her sister's disappearance. A man couldn't help but wonder if she would bring that same kind of enthusiasm and energy to his bed.

It was only as the applause broke out that Holt realized he wasn't the only man who was appreciating Carly's boxing form. Nor was he the only one, he imagined, who was thinking of getting her into bed.

He could almost feel something inside him snap as a wave of jealousy rolled through him. It wasn't rational. Like most of the other emotions Carly pulled out of him, it was basic, primitive, raw. Knowing that didn't prevent him from striding toward the stairs.

When he heard her laugh at something the trainer said, he clenched his hands into fists. He'd taken three steps down the stairs when he saw the man dig a notebook out of his gym bag and scribble something. Carly took the paper he tore off.

Then, amid the hoots and whistles of the small group of men who had gathered around, she threw her arms around the trainer and hugged him before blithely making her way to the stairs. She seemed totally unaware that the men couldn't seem to take their eyes off her as she climbed to meet him.

"I've got it," she said, waving the paper at him.

Holt took it from her and stuffed it into his pocket before he rushed her up the rest of the stairs, bundled her into her coat and hurried her out onto the street. The doors were still swinging shut behind them when he urged her toward the wall of the building, out of the way of pedestrians, and said, "Before we go anywhere, we're going to get something straight."

"You're angry," Carly said, searching his face. "Why? Sal gave me a name and an address."

"Sal?" Even as he watched, some of the excitement left her eyes, to be replaced by confusion and then curiosity. The fact that the analytical part of her mind was still operational, that she could look at him in that cool way as if he were a beetle in a jar while he badly wanted to punch something, only made him angrier. "Your father has made me responsible for your safety. And as long as I am, I expect you to obey a reasonable order when I give one."

Carly's eyebrows shot up. "And which reasonable order of yours did I disobey?"

Holt's jaw tightened. "I told you to stay put."

"Are you saying I disobeyed that order? When—" she poked a finger into his chest "—was I out of your sight for even one minute while we were in there?" She poked him again. "Did I leave the premises at any time?"

She was angry, too. He could see it in the way her chin had lifted and her eyes had darkened. That gave him some satisfaction. But she was still capable of logic while his hands had curled into fists. That made him furious.

"I told you before," Carly said as she poked him a third time, "I'm not a child. Don't order me around like one."

The last time he'd felt overwhelmed by the need to pop someone in the chin, he'd been a kid fighting for survival in the playground. But he wasn't a child anymore. Neither one of them was. Control. He thought of it briefly, then tossed it away. Grabbing her by the shoulders, he closed the small distance between them and covered her mouth with his.

Shoppers hurried by on the crowded sidewalk. Raised eyebrows, muffled laughter went unnoticed. Not even a strident wolf whistle could penetrate the world they created together.

His kiss was everything she'd remembered—hot, fierce, demanding—and more. Her back was pressed against the building, held there by the firm, hard lines of his body. She was trapped. But she didn't want to go anywhere. All she wanted was to be here, she thought as she slipped her hands beneath his jacket, running them up the smooth planes and muscles of his back.

She should push him away. She should at least try to think. But her hands gripped him tighter, and her mind was already dimming, narrowing like the spotlight on a stage until it was focused only on Holt and the way he could make her feel.

Everything. Each sensation was so sharp, so clear. His teeth scraped against her lip and sent a bolt of pleasure through her. His hand, hard and urgent, left a trail of fire as it slipped beneath her coat to move in one possessive stroke from her hip to her breast. When he changed the angle of the kiss, she tasted the fierce, demanding flavor of his need. Irresistible.

She was driving him crazy. Slowly, he drew his hand down her side to her hip and then back up again. It seemed he'd waited forever to touch her. Her skin was much softer than he'd imagined. And the thin material of the spandex was tempting, maddening. He ached to have her out of it.

In some part of his mind that hadn't yet shut down, Holt knew that he was kissing her in the middle of a Manhattan street. But he couldn't seem to stop. As the taste of her surrender poured into him, he drew her closer, molding the curves of her body to his. He cursed himself for acting like a senseless teenager, then cursed her for driving him to it.

But in another part of his mind, he knew that he'd wanted this for a very long time. It seemed he'd been waiting forever to touch her. To hold her. To discover she was everything he wanted. All that he wanted. Impossible.

He was standing on solid concrete, but what he felt beneath his feet were separate particles of sand, shifting, ebbing. With her taste filling him and the fire in her body leaping to his, Holt struggled to keep his balance. In another moment, he'd be swept up in the undertow. Unless he moved now...

He wasn't steady. That was his first coherent thought when he managed to pull away. He kept his hands on the building on either side of her for a moment, until the earth stopped tilting. It gave him little satisfaction to see that she looked as stunned as he felt. Her eyes were wide and clouded, and they'd darkened to the color of very old brandy. Her hands were cupped around her elbows, and for the first time since he'd met her, she looked defenseless, vulnerable. Holt cursed himself again, then turned and with a sharp whistle brought a taxi to the curb. Though he didn't trust himself to touch her, he followed close behind her to the cab.

ONCE INSIDE THE TAXI, Holt fished the paper Carly had handed him out of his pocket and read it to the driver. Then he leaned back, bracing himself as the car shot away from the curb. Neither he nor Carly spoke. They didn't even look at each other. Holt stared out the window. Most of yesterday's snowfall had been cleared from the streets, and the traffic... The cab lurched to a sudden stop and the driver simultaneously pounded on his horn, shouted in a foreign language at the car ahead, then managed to wedge his vehicle between two cars in the next lane. Tires squealed. More horns blasted. Traffic had returned to normal, Holt decided.

At the first signal light, he risked a glance at Carly. They were seated as far apart as they could possibly get in the back seat of the taxi. Under other circumstances, Holt might have been amused. But there wasn't much in their present situation that he found funny.

The truth was, he wanted Carly Carpenter more than he'd wanted any woman. Each time he kissed her, he wanted her more.

But there was a whole list of reasons why he couldn't just reach out and take what he wanted where Carly was concerned.

Right at the top was her offer to become his bride. Obviously he couldn't take Calvin Carpenter's daughter to bed and then not marry her. And marrying Carly...well, it was out of the question. He'd agreed to marry Jenna because Calvin had insisted, and because he could have compartmentalized his relationship with her into a nice, convenient corner of his life.

Marrying Carly would be like somersaulting off the bar of a flying trapeze with no safety net. He had no doubt she'd find a way to push herself into every facet of his life just as she'd pushed her way into every part of his mind.

She pulled at his emotions in a way that he hadn't allowed anyone to do since he'd lost his parents. Worst of all, she undermined his control. For a moment there, when he'd been kissing her, he'd lost track of where they were, why they were there, everything.

He couldn't afford to let that happen again. He'd promised Calvin that he'd keep her safe.

Safe? Less than an hour ago she'd nearly been run down by a car. Even as the image slipped into his mind, he recalled the sharp twist of fear, the numbing helplessness he'd experienced.

And the blue car. Holt suddenly realized that he hadn't even thought to look for it when he'd hurried her into the taxi. Twisting in his seat, he scanned the traffic and spotted one, three cars back, too far to be sure it was the same car that had nearly run her down.

Unless it followed them.

Leaning forward, he tapped the driver on the shoulder. "Take us through Central Park on the way to that address, will you?" When the driver nodded, Holt took a quick look through the rear window again. Only time would tell if they were being tailed.

Either way, for both their sakes, he couldn't let Carly distract him again. Turning, he let his gaze rest on her.

She'd taken the gauze off her knuckles and clasped her hands together tightly in her lap. Holt took some comfort in the fact that she was obviously as bothered by what had happened as he was. All he could see was her profile, but he knew if she turned to face him, he'd see that little line on her forehead, the one that always appeared when she was thinking.

If she wasn't in the back seat of a taxi, she'd be pacing, trying to come up with a solution. The same solution that he was seeking, he bet. He could almost hear the wheels turning. And in the back of her mind, she was probably reviewing notes she'd jotted down on one of her cards. Even as he imagined it, he was strongly tempted to break her concentration. All it would take was a touch. Running a finger along her jaw ought to do it. Very carefully, Holt folded his hands in his lap and quickly reviewed in his own mind all the reasons why he shouldn't touch Carly Carpenter again.

Carly had her hands clasped so tightly together they had begun to ache. But if she relaxed them, they just might begin to tremble again.

For the first few moments after she'd slid ahead of Holt into the back seat of the cab, she'd concentrated on taking deep breaths. It was the best method she knew to get oxygen to her brain. Oxygen was essential for thinking, and she badly needed to think.

She remembered the note card in her pocket, outlining her plan to attract Holt Cassidy. Well, she'd certainly succeeded. She didn't need a Ph.D. after her name to recognize desire when it jumped out and grabbed her by the throat.

The problem was that she'd succeeded in making herself want him, too. Obviously the proximity thing worked two ways. She'd have to remember to make note of that. Perhaps that was why she'd failed dismally to keep him at arm's length.

She thought again of what it had felt like to have his body pressed against hers, his hands moving over her. Nothing in her research had prepared her for the flood of emotions he'd set loose in her.

And she hadn't done one thing to stop him. He'd been the one who pulled away. He'd even whistled for a taxi. She couldn't even purse her lips. What was wrong with her?

Could this be what it was like to fall in love?

No!

The taxi skidded to a stop at a traffic light. Carly barely kept herself from getting out and running away.

She *wasn't* in love! She'd taken enough courses in psychology to know that sexual attraction was often mistaken for love. Women had a long history of frequently confusing the two. She knew better than to do that. Didn't she?

Carly swallowed a sigh. She also knew better than to try to analyze love. Or to try to confine its components to a note card. Love was mysterious, elusive. It defied logic.

Deep inside of her, she was pretty sure she *was* in love. She'd probably been in love with Holt Cassidy from the first moment she'd met him, undeniably from that mad moment when she'd agreed to Jenna's plan. Oh, she'd made up plenty of excuses, but it was more than the ticking of her biological clock that had made her go to his apartment that morning.

And it was a whole lot more than simple biology making her feel breathless and giddy...and scared out of her wits right now!

And she didn't have a single clue what to do next. Only that she couldn't let Holt know what she was feeling. He already had far too much power over her. More than ever before, it was important that she keep on an even footing with him. And that required keeping her distance.

"Well, have you figured it out yet?" Holt asked.

Carly turned to face him. "No...but I...I mean we..."

"You're stuttering," Holt said.

Carly's chin shot up. "I have a plan."

"Somehow, I was *sure* that you would."

Carly's eyes narrowed. His lips had definitely twitched. "Was that a wisecrack?"

Holt sighed. "What do you suppose my problem is—my timing or my delivery?"

"Neither," Carly shot back dryly. "When it comes to kissing, you're up to speed on both." Then she felt the heat flood her cheeks as she realized what she'd said.

Holt chuckled, then burst out laughing. Carly struggled for a moment, then joined him. The sound had the cabbie grinning and muttering something incomprehensible over his shoulder.

"It really isn't funny," Carly said finally. "And there's only one solution that I can think of. We just can't kiss again. Agreed?"

"Surely you've heard the one about good intentions and the path to perdition," he said.

"I said I had a plan." Carly prayed that she did.

"If you think about it, what happened back there on the sidewalk was fueled as much by anger as by..."

"Mutual desire," Holt suggested.

"Right. But what I'm saying is, when it comes right down to it, you kissed me because you were mad at me. Why?"

"I wasn't mad at you. Exactly. I just don't like it when someone tries to run down my partner. Besides, you were mad, too."

"Because *I* don't like it when someone orders me around," Carly explained. "And you have a habit of doing that. Probably because you're a CEO. When I told you my plan about handling Father Finelli, you dismissed it. And at the gym, first you told me to follow you around and take notes, then you told me to stay put. You didn't even ask my advice. If you had, I would have suggested that it would be more efficient to question the trainer."

"I thought it might be more discreet to ask someone else. I didn't want to alert Jenna's personal trainer to the fact that she was missing. And from where I was standing, it looked more like you were flirting than questioning," Holt said.

"Yes." Carly smiled. "It's the first time I ever tried it, and I was good at it, wasn't I?"

"What you were was lucky," Holt said.

"Sal was very charming."

Holt leaned closer. "Carly, you were in a crowded gym. If Sal could have got you alone, that charm might have worn very thin, very quickly."

"Well, he didn't. It didn't." Suddenly she realized that they were practically nose to nose. Drawing back, she continued, "And we have to stop arguing. All it does is cause friction. So that means you have to stop giving arbitrary orders. From now on, we have to discuss things and reach a mutually agreeable solution." It sounded good, Carly thought as she wound up her totally extemporaneous little speech. It might even work.

Holt glanced quickly out the rear window as the taxi turned into Central Park. Then he turned back to Carly. "And what if we can't agree? In the end, someone has to make the decision. Especially if it means life or death."

"That's the CEO talking. I'm not your employee. I'm your partner, so we'll take turns," Carly said. "One time, you call the shots, the next time, I do. Agreed?"

"Agreed." Then, in a movement too swift for her to avoid it, Holt reached out and took her chin in his hand. "*Except* when your safety is involved. Then I give the orders and you follow them."

"I don't see—"

"Take a look out the window and you will." He turned her chin. "See that blue car? It's the same color

The Editor's "Thank You" Free Gifts Include:

- Two BRAND-NEW romance novels!
- An exciting mystery gift!

PLACE FREE GIFT SEAL HERE

YES! I have placed my Editor's "Thank You" seal in the space provided above. Please send me 2 free books and an exciting mystery gift. I understand I am under no obligation to purchase any books, as explained on the back and on the opposite page.

142 HDL CF3E (U-H-T-03/98)

Name _____

Address _____ Apt. _____

City _____

State _____ Zip _____

Thank You!

DETACH AND MAIL CARD TODAY!

Harlequin Reader Service® — Here's How It Works:

Accepting free books places you under no obligation to buy anything. You may keep the books and gift and return the shipping statement marked "cancel." If you do not cancel, about a month later we will send you 4 additional novels, and bill you just $3.12 each plus 25¢ delivery per book and applicable sales tax, if any.* That's the complete price, and—compared to cover prices of $3.75 each—quite a bargain! You may cancel at any time, but if you choose to continue, every month we'll send you 4 more books, which you may either purchase at the discount price...or return to us and cancel your subscription.
*Terms and prices subject to change without notice. Sales tax applicable in N.Y.

BUSINESS REPLY MAIL
FIRST-CLASS MAIL   PERMIT NO. 717   BUFFALO, NY

POSTAGE WILL BE PAID BY ADDRESSEE

HARLEQUIN READER SERVICE
3010 WALDEN AVE
PO BOX 1867
BUFFALO NY 14240-9952

NO POSTAGE
NECESSARY
IF MAILED
IN THE
UNITED STATES

and make as the one that nearly ran you down, and it's been following us since we left the gym."

Releasing her, he turned to the cab driver. "Take a right onto Central Park South, and let us off across from the Plaza Hotel."

Carly kept her eyes on the blue car while the taxi careened around two corners and lurched to a stop at the curb.

Holt paid the driver, then turned back to her, resting one finger beneath her chin. "We can take turns calling the shots, Carly. But you'd better remember that boxing lesson and keep your guard up. All the rules in the world don't change the fact that I want to make love to you, and you want it, too."

Carly stared at him as he got out of the cab. It was just as well she didn't have any note cards with her. She had a funny feeling that the solution she'd proposed wouldn't have been worth the paper she would have written it on.

6

THE MOMENT THEY WERE both out of the taxi, Carly risked a quick glance at the blue car. Caught by the light, it hadn't made the right turn onto Central Park South. She spotted two people in the front seat before Holt took her arm and hurried her along the street past a line of hansom cabs. The cold, snowy weather was slowing down the demand for the horse-drawn carriages. Drivers were chatting, blowing on their hands. Across the street, she could see quite a crowd gathered in front of the Plaza Hotel, tourists opting for the kind of cabs that had heaters.

"Where are we going?" Carly asked as they reached the corner.

"On a little detour," Holt said. "I'd prefer we didn't have company when we visit Lance's apartment." The instant the light turned, he urged her across the street.

As soon as they reached the curb and headed toward the hotel, Carly glanced across the street. She saw the dark blue car wedge its way between two hansom cabs. Her stomach sank as someone got out. A small man, wearing a black ski cap and dark clothes. He was trying to cross in the middle of the block. There was a squeal of tires, a rising crescendo of horns. Then Holt was pulling her through the glass-doored entrance to the hotel.

She had to run to keep up with him as he hurried her

across the lobby. The last time she'd been to the Plaza was two years ago. She was about to leave for Manilai, and Jenna and her father had treated her to a long, leisurely brunch in the Palm Court. Today, she could barely hear the violins as they raced past it.

When Holt paused for a moment at the entrance to the Oak Room, she glanced around the lobby. It was crowded. She couldn't see the man in the ski cap.

She was still searching when Holt gripped her hand. "C'mon." He ran interference until they were at the center of a throng of people heading out the side entrance. Seconds later, a revolving door shot them out into the street.

Two tour buses waited at the curb. Holt kept a tight grip on her hand as they ducked between them, single file, then dodged their way around cars until they reached the opposite curb. She was out of breath when he finally drew her into a small restaurant on the corner. The air was warm and rich with the scent of coffee and cinnamon.

A harried hostess managed a smile. "Table for two?"

"Could we see a menu, please?" Holt asked. "My wife has allergies."

Menu in hand, he drew her to a coat rack near the plate glass windows, which afforded a view of two streets.

"Okay," she said. "What's the game plan? I've never in my life had an allergy to coffee or cinnamon buns. And that seems to be their specialty."

"We didn't come in here to eat," Holt said. "While I pretend to check out the menu, you're going to make sure we're not being followed."

"Aye, aye, sir." But when she tried to move past him to the window, he stepped in her way.

"You can't get too close. They're looking for us, too."

"Right." Edging a little closer to him, she peered past his shoulder. Even with the coat rack partially blocking her view, she could see pedestrians lining up at the corner, then pouring into the street. The moment she spotted the ski cap, she gripped Holt's arm. "I see him, I think. He's talking on a cellular phone."

"Look for the blue car," Holt said. "See if you can get a license plate number."

Carly waited, watching. Because of the coat rack, she couldn't see the cars until they reached the corner. Then she nearly missed it because one of the tour buses pulled out. "Z-Q...damn! It turned the corner, and the bus is blocking my view." Minutes went by as the large tour bus slowly inched its way through the intersection. By the time it was gone, there wasn't a sign of the blue car. "They're gone," she said.

The disappointment in her voice had Holt glancing down at her in amusement. "That's good news, Carly. We were trying to give them the slip."

"Well, I'd like to give them a few other things, including a piece of my mind," she said.

"And perhaps that left jab you were working on?" he asked with a laugh.

"You can count on it," she replied.

Reaching out, he ran a finger down her earring. "You'll have your revenge in good time. Haven't you heard it's a dish best eaten cold?" Taking her hand again, he led the way through the restaurant toward an alternate exit. "In the meantime, they may circle around a few times to see if they can pick us up again. Follow me."

And follow him she did. Down a series of streets, some narrow and choked with delivery trucks, others

teeming with cars and people. Past countless buildings, a few with ornate facades and awnings, even
doormen, others with homeless people huddled in
entranceways and beneath stairwells. He even led her
through a short alley, ripe with the smell of stale beer
and rotting garbage, before he stopped in the middle of
a busy block.

"Chinese or Italian?" he asked. At her puzzled look,
he continued. "We need to discuss what we want to do
next. There's a Chinese restaurant across the street, an
Italian one on this side. I can vouch for both. And unless you're deathly allergic to one cuisine or the other,
your safety's not an issue. So it's your call, partner."

Carly's eyes narrowed instantly. "You're just doing
this so that you get to decide what our next move is.
That's not—"

"You set up the rules. If we don't abide by them, we
could have another argument in the middle of the
street. We both know where that could lead."

He was smiling at her, and it just wasn't fair that she
wanted to smile back. Then it dawned on her that two
could play his game. "Italian. They invented espresso."

"You won't be disappointed," he promised as he led
the way to the restaurant.

"You can count on it," she said.

She didn't regret her choice. The small, cozy restaurant provided a feast for the senses. In a corner near a
curved mahogany bar, a fountain spilled water over
rocks into a small pond. Round, golden cheeses hung
from the ceiling, and the hot, spicy aromas lingering in
the air had her mouth watering.

The lunchtime crowd was starting to thin, and wait-
ers were hurriedly resetting tables and refilling coffee

cups. One of them spotted Holt and hurried to greet him with a warm handshake. Moments later, they were seated in a booth, listening to the day's specials.

"What can I bring you?" The waiter turned expectantly to Carly.

"Your call, partner." She smiled sweetly at Holt.

"The special vegetarian pizza."

Carly made a face at him. "I'm going to gag if it has sprouts on it."

"You can make the call, if you prefer," Holt offered.

Carly shook her head.

"And to drink?" the waiter asked.

Holt looked at her inquiringly.

"No way," she said. "It's still your call." Then she braced herself for the order.

"Two herbal teas. Carpenter's Spring Delight, if you have it."

Carly winced, then leaned back to study Holt. "You practice what you preach, don't you?"

"Pardon?"

"You're about to take over a health food conglomerate, and you actually believe in it. You drink the teas." She shook her head. "Even in an Italian restaurant, you order healthy food. Carpenter Enterprises is more than just a business to you."

"It's very definitely a business, and it earns a good profit."

"But it means more than money to you."

"Don't turn me into something I'm not, Carly. I warned you before, I'm not nice."

She leaned forward. "No, you're not." *Nice* was much too bland a word to describe Holt Cassidy. "I haven't quite figured it out yet. But running a corporation isn't the only thing you're good at. You gave those guys in the blue car the slip as if you'd been doing that kind of thing all your life. Don't tell me you learned that in business school."

"Another study, Carly?" He pushed a napkin toward her. "They don't have note cards here. But I imagine this will do in a pinch."

"Sorry." She raised her hands, palms out. "I'll back off." *For now.* She said the words silently as the waiter delivered their tea. And she'd lied about being sorry, too. She was going to figure out exactly what made Holt Cassidy tick. She had to if she was ever going to hold her own with him. Leaning back, she watched Holt perform the ritual of pouring hot water over the tea bag in the cup. Even at a distance, the stuff smelled like a meadow.

"Aren't you even going to try yours?" Holt asked.

She stifled a shudder. "After that Celery-Asparagus Surprise, I think I've had my quota of green liquids for the day. One more swallow and I might turn into Kermit the Frog."

Shaking his head, Holt signaled the waiter. "Bring the lady a cappuccino."

Carly's eyes widened in surprise.

"I'm not being nice," Holt said. "It's a bribe. As soon as we finish eating, I want to take you back to the penthouse."

"Absolutely not. The next move's my call. And I say we visit Lance's apartment."

Holt sipped his tea, then set it down. "It's a matter of safety, Carly, and you agreed—"

"Fine, let's talk about my safety. You said yourself, I'm safer with you."

"I couldn't do anything about that car. It nearly ran you down."

Carly waved a hand. "You took care of it the second time. We gave them the slip. And think of your list of suspects. Tom, Mark, Danny—they're all at the Carpenter Building. I'm not going to be safe there, either, until we find out what's going on."

The hell of it was, she was right, Holt thought as the waiter served the cappuccino. And when she was backed into a corner, she fought with the same ferocity that her father did. And with the same razor-sharp logic. He wondered if she realized how very much alike they were.

"I'll agree to a compromise," he said. "We'll go to Lance's apartment, but I'll send two of the security people to his office. He listed Sterling Securities as his employer on his membership card." He took a sip of his tea. "Who knew you were going to visit Jenna's health club?"

"Susan Masterson. She knew I was going to visit Father Finelli, too. She helped me find the phone number."

"As Jenna's secretary, she would be the most likely person to have discovered Jenna was having an affair," Holt pointed out. "Would Jenna have confided in her?"

Carly shook her head. "She's not the kind of woman who invites confidences. She's cool, detached. But she could have noticed something." She frowned. "It's not as though we can just come right out and ask her."

"Who else knew where you were going?"

"I ran into Mark and Tom and Danny when they got off the elevator. They were asking about Jenna, so I told them I was off to the gym to keep her appointment. The only person I didn't personally blab it to is Sam Waterman. And I'm not ready to eliminate him as a

suspect. Someone could be keeping him informed."
Carly sighed. "I might as well have taken out an ad in
the *New York Times*."

"Your father and I knew, too, Carly."

Carly stared at Holt. "Surely you're not suggest-
ing—" She waited for the waiter to serve the pizza and
then leaned toward Holt. "You can't suspect my father."

He met her eyes steadily. "You're too trusting. I
think you ought to suspect everyone."

She thought it through for the length of time it took
her to work her way through half a slice of pizza. Then
she folded her arms on the table. "You and my father
are *not* on my list of suspects. It goes against logic. Dad
has no motive. If he didn't want you to get control of
the company and marry Jenna, he could have prevented it without kidnapping his own daughter—or
arranging for her to be seduced. And you don't want to
ruin Carpenter Enterprises. You want to take it into the
twenty-first century. Badly enough to agree to marry
my sister when you would have preferred not to."

"Perhaps I arranged the kidnapping or orchestrated
the elopement so that I could get control of Carpenter
Enterprises without having to marry her," Holt said. "I
couldn't have foreseen that she'd talk you into taking
her place. Now you're the one standing in my way.
You shouldn't trust me, Carly."

His voice was cold enough to send a shiver up her
spine. Even his eyes had frosted over. Here was the
menace, the ruthlessness she'd sensed from the first.
Here was the corporate shark. The hunter. There was a
violence in him, but he was careful to control it. Lifting
the cappuccino, she took a sip. There was a wellspring
of kindness in him, too, as much as he might want to

deny it. And he didn't scare her one bit. Her eyes were perfectly steady when they met his. "But I do. I trust you."

Three words. How could those three simple words have brought on the flood of emotions he felt pouring through him? He'd been prepared for her withdrawal. He'd been hoping for it. He'd even braced himself to see the fear in her eyes. But he hadn't been ready for her trust. And it was changing him. He could feel something inside of him melting, washing away like water. "Carly..."

She raised a hand. "You're not going to change my mind, so we might as well move on to what we're going to do once we get to Lance's apartment. What in the world was his last name anyway? You grabbed that piece of paper Sal gave me before I had a chance to look at it."

"Bigelow, I think," Holt said as he reached in his pocket.

"It can't be," Carly said.

Holt smoothed the paper out and laid it on the table.

"Lance Bigelow." Carly stared at the scribbled name. "It can't be a coincidence." Looking up, she met Holt's eyes. "I know him. It's Jenna's Lancelot. I should have put it together sooner. Lance...Lancelot. It's not like it's a common name."

"Who is Jenna's Lancelot?" Holt asked.

"Her knight in shining armor. The boy she was in love with when she was a junior in high school. His last name was Bigelow. She always called him Lancelot. I think she thought of herself as Guinevere. It's the French version of Jennifer. And they did turn out to be star-crossed lovers. They wanted to get married. But my father prevented it. A week after graduation, Lance and his family disappeared. I tried to find them. I even went behind my father's back and hired a private detective. He couldn't find a trace. It was as if they'd gone into some witness protection program. Jenna was heartbroken. And—" Carly raised her hands and dropped them "—I couldn't do a thing to help her."

"Is that why you felt you had to help her this time?" Holt asked.

"No...well, yes, I suppose that was part of it. If this is the same Lancelot, no wonder she didn't want anyone to know. She didn't even tell *me*."

"Tit for tat," Holt murmured. "If this Lance is the same lover Jenna had in high school, and Calvin interfered, he could be out for revenge."

"But he loved Jenna. And she loved him, too. And if they're lucky enough to have found each other after all these years...he can't have Jenna and revenge, too. And Jenna wouldn't betray her family."

"You're looking for a fairy-tale ending," Holt said. "In real life they don't exist."

"There's only one solution," Carly said. "We'll go to his apartment and see what his neighbors can tell us about him."

"LOOK, LADY, I mind my own business. Why don't you mind yours?"

Carly sighed in frustration as the short, balding man who'd been glaring at her through the two-inch crack permitted by the security chain firmly shut the door in her face. He'd been more polite, but no more informative, than the other tenants in the converted brownstone where Lance Bigelow lived on the second floor.

Under other circumstances, Carly would have been intrigued, fascinated even, by the isolated lives that

New Yorkers carved out for themselves while they lived in one of the most densely populated cities in the world. It would make an interesting study.

But the truth was, she wanted to scream. So far the only information Lance's neighbors had provided was that he paid his rent on time. The superintendent had testified to that but claimed he'd never seen Mr. Bigelow in person. The address in the Upper East Sixties spoke of at least moderate affluence, and the scaffolding on the outside of the building indicated that the landlords cared about preserving the architecture. So Lance Bigelow wasn't living in a hovel.

Who was she kidding? So far, they'd discovered absolutely zip. Holt had warned her during the ride over that Manhattan wasn't Manilai. And he'd been right. Not that she'd been expecting the friendliness that permeated the villages on her South Seas island. But there were only six apartments in the building, and she'd been hoping that one of them housed someone who knew Lance Bigelow well.

Turning to Holt, she said, "Go ahead. Say it. Your security people could have discovered more."

"Actually, I don't think they could have," Holt said. And he meant it. He'd enjoyed watching her pull information out of the superintendent. There wasn't a doubt in his mind that she was excellent at what she called "field research." It had taken real talent laced with dogged determination to keep the sour-faced old scrooge talking for almost ten minutes. An essential part of her charm was that she seemed genuinely interested in whoever she was questioning. And she was. If the guy had known anything else, he would have gladly spilled it.

Lifting her chin with his finger, Holt said, "I warned

you. New Yorkers keep to themselves. But they do tend to make social contacts at work. I'm sure the security team will have more luck at Sterling Securities."

"And in the meantime?" Carly asked.

"We go back to your father's office and wait for them to report in." Holt led her down the flight of stairs to the entrance. On the stoop, they found their way blocked by a small, elderly woman with a wild mop of reddish orange hair that almost matched the color of her high-top sneakers. One of the two Dobermans she held on a leash growled deep in its throat.

"Hush up, Gawain," she said as she backed down the steps, pulling the dogs with her. "These two aren't muggers. And they don't have bulging briefcases, so I don't think they're salespeople, either." She glanced back up at Holt and Carly. "I'm giving you fair warning. These dogs have been trained to kill muggers and anyone who wants to sell me things I don't need."

Carly smiled at the woman as she extended her hand to the dog that hadn't growled. "We're not selling anything."

When the Doberman licked her hand, Carly began to pet its head. "I bet this one is named after the Green Knight."

"Familiar with the Arthurian legend, are you?" the woman asked as she gave them another quick once-over. "Not many young people are anymore. Proof positive that the whole American education system has gone down the tubes."

"Actually, we're here on a quest," Holt explained with a smile. "We're looking for Lance Bigelow."

"Suspected as much," the woman said, turning her attention to Holt. "They warned me the wicked father would come asking questions. Merlin with an evil streak—that's my nickname for him. But you're not old enough to be him. Though you've got the eyes of a Merlin." Her own eyes narrowed slightly. "I guess that leaves King Arthur, although with a smile like that, you shouldn't have had any trouble keeping Guinevere at your side."

"Then you do know Lance?" Carly asked.

"Well enough to be baby-sitting his dogs," the woman replied. Signaling them to sit down, she settled herself on the flat edge of the cement balustrade.

"I'm Jenna's sister, Carly, and this is Holt Cassidy," Carly explained.

"Molly Lieberman," the woman said, "and you've already met the two knights."

"We know Jenna's eloped with Lance Bigelow," Carly said. "Can you tell us where they've gone?"

"My lips are sealed," the woman replied, then pantomimed turning a key in front of her mouth and tossing it away. "But if you want my opinion, it's the smartest thing your sister's done. True love's a precious commodity in this life. You gotta reach out and grab it. Instead of trying to stop them, you ought to be happy for them."

"You don't understand. We're not trying to ruin the elopement," Carly explained. "But my father's received a note that Jenna's been kidnapped."

"Carly—" Holt began.

She glanced quickly at him, then turned her attention back to Molly. "You won't tell the newspapers, will you?"

When the woman pantomimed turning the key and tossing it away again, Carly poured out the whole story. She was nearly finished when the two dogs began barking and pulling at their leashes.

"Hush up." Rising, the woman calmed the dogs, whose attention had become riveted on the corner of the building where the scaffolding hung. "What's the matter with you? Muggers don't hang out on roofs. They like alleys or deserted parks," she admonished them. Then she shifted her attention back to Carly and Holt. "I can tell you one thing. Your sister and Lance weren't kidnapped. Drove 'em to the airport myself."

"That doesn't mean that someone didn't intercept them when they reached their destination," Carly said. "Please tell us where they've gone."

"They didn't tell me. Claimed they didn't tell anyone. My advice to the two of you is to go home, relax and wait for the happy ending."

"The ending wasn't so happy for the real Lancelot and Guinevere," Holt pointed out.

"Because they got caught," the woman said as she urged the dogs up the steps. "Lancelot Bigelow's too smart to let evil Merlin spoil things the second time around. Come to think of it— " she turned back to Carly "—this whole kidnapping hoax could be a ploy by your father to find out where they are so that he can ruin things again. Think about it. He doesn't come here himself. Instead, he's got the two of you playing detective. I wouldn't have told *him* a thing. But if I knew anything, I might just have spilled my guts to a handsome guy like you." She winked at Holt before she turned and walked into the building.

As soon as the door clicked shut behind her, Carly whirled to face Holt. "My father is not behind this. He's not evil. He...he just wouldn't..."

Holt reached for her hands. "I don't think he's behind it, either, Carly. For one thing, he wouldn't do anything to put you or your sister in danger. And

Molly's scenario doesn't explain the fact that someone wants to get hold of the tea formula."

"No," Carly agreed. She could hang on to that. And then she realized that she was hanging on to Holt, too, gripping his hands tightly. For a moment, she didn't let go. "I was so sure we'd learn something here. But we're not getting anywhere. We're not any closer to finding Jenna than we were last night."

"We know the name of the man she eloped with. And there may be news waiting for us right now back at your father's office. We're going to find her, Carly." Even as he said the words, he wanted to take them back. He was making a promise that he wasn't sure he could keep. She'd pulled it out of him. No, that wasn't true. He'd given it freely.

Holt knew he should step away, but he didn't. He was only holding her hands. But he could see everything she was feeling in her eyes. And what he'd said had eased the fear that had sprung into them only seconds before. He couldn't have named the emotions that moved through him. Something was happening here. He was changing, losing ground. Lowering his head, he brushed his lips against hers and lost more.

This was different, so different from the other kisses they'd shared. Where was the sharp twist of desire, the molten fire in his blood? What was this warmth, sweet and sure, spreading through him? He deepened the kiss, slowly, seeking more, wanting it all. No one had ever made him feel this way. *Needed.* The moment the word drifted through his mind, he felt fear slice through him. Being needed was the last thing he wanted. It was everything he wanted.

Carly felt herself tumbling, free-falling. This kiss was so different. She felt none of the urgency, none of the demand of the earlier ones. And still it was destroying her. She could feel his emotions pouring through her, the desire, the fear and above all the quiet beginnings of joy. She recognized each one, because she was feeling it, too. And it was suddenly too much.

They drew back at the same moment, but neither one of them spoke. Holt kept his arm around her shoulders as they turned without speaking and headed toward the corner.

Afterward, he wasn't sure what warned him. Whether it was the shout from across the street or the sudden change in the light overhead. In nightmares, he would even hear the creak of the boards overhead. And he would forever wonder if it was fast reflexes or a miracle that caused him to tighten his grip on Carly and lunge toward the safety of the wall. All he could clearly remember later was watching the concrete chunk smash and splinter into fragments on the sidewalk where they'd been standing only seconds earlier.

7

HOLDING CARLY TIGHTLY against him, Holt leaned back against the building and forced himself to breathe as he stared at the sidewalk. He could still hear the sound of the concrete shattering. He could still see the block cracking and splattering on impact. His gaze followed a small piece that was rolling away until it finally dropped off the curb into the street.

If Carly had been standing there, if he hadn't pulled her away... Even as the image pushed its way into his mind, he shoved it out and tightened his hold on her.

"Hey, are you two all right?"

Holt shifted his gaze to the elderly man hurrying toward them. "We're fine." Saying the words helped to drown out the noise that he couldn't seem to stop hearing.

The man shook his head as he looked at the smashed chunk of concrete. "Won't do any good to call the police. He'll be half a mile away by now. But something should be done."

"Who'll be half a mile away?" Holt asked.

"The guy on the roof. I was sitting on my stoop having a smoke. My wife don't allow it in our apartment. And I saw him. He was wearing one of those tight-fitting hats, what d'ya call them?"

"Ski caps," Holt murmured, drawing Carly with

him as he stepped away from the building so that he could see the roof.

"Ain't up there now," the man said. "Took off the minute he dropped that chunk of stone. These roofs are so close together, he'll be a couple blocks away by now." He shook his head. "We usually don't have this kind of malicious mischief in the neighborhood. You could have been hurt."

"Thanks for warning us," Holt said.

"Yes, thank you," Carly added.

"Don't mention it." The man nodded at them, then turned to Holt. "Your lady looks like she could use a drink. I can vouch for the bar up two blocks and around the corner."

"Thanks." Holt tightened his grip on Carly and drew her past the crumbled piece of concrete. It was two blocks before he spotted a taxi.

When he whistled for it, Carly said, "I thought we were going to get a drink."

"We'll get it back at the Carpenter Building," Holt replied as he opened the door of the cab.

"Don't I get a say in this?"

"No. That rock almost landed on your head. Since this is clearly a matter of safety, I'm taking you back to your father. If you want to argue in the back seat of a taxi, you do so at your own risk."

Carly climbed into the car without another word. Partly because those were the rules she'd agreed to. But mostly because when a person called a spade a spade, it was hard to argue. Besides, she'd learned a long time ago in dealing with her father the value of a strategic retreat. It wouldn't do her a bit of good to discuss anything with Holt right now. One look at the implacable expression on his face told her that.

And then there was the unarguable fact that whoever had dropped the rock couldn't have been sure
which one of them it would hit. It didn't take a rocket
scientist to conclude that the person didn't much care.
She felt another layer of ice form over the ball of fear
that had settled in her stomach.

As soon as the taxi had turned into traffic, she risked
a glance at Holt. She wondered if he'd reached the
same conclusion, that his life was in danger, too. All
she could tell from looking at him was that he was
withdrawing, isolating himself again.

And why not? Like King Arthur, his kingdom, his
dream for the future, was crumbling around him the
same way that chunk of concrete had shattered when it
smashed into the sidewalk. Just thinking about it had
the coppery taste of fear rising again in her throat. And
she knew as clearly as she knew her own name that the
fear had every bit as much to do with the fact that Holt
was going to draw away from her as it had to do with
a falling rock.

When the taxi pulled up to the entrance of the Carpenter Building, Holt grabbed her arm to keep her in
the cab until he'd paid the driver. Once on the sidewalk, he urged her toward the doors, but she stopped
short.

"Carly—" he began.

"Look across the street," she said in a low voice. "In
front of the coffee shop."

Holt looked over. Sam Waterman was talking ear-
nestly to Susan Masterson. When Susan spotted them,
she waved and hurried toward them. Sam saluted
them with his hat before he turned and entered the
shop.

"What's Sam Waterman doing here?" Holt asked as soon as Susan reached them.

"He stopped by to see Mr. Carpenter," Susan replied. "He was just asking me about Jenna. But I didn't know what to tell him." She turned to Carly. "Your sister's wedding dress arrived. They delivered it to the office by mistake, and I took it up to her personally. I thought it might cheer her up. But the security guard wouldn't let me through. Has her condition worsened?"

"No." Carly smiled at Susan. "My father doesn't want her to be disturbed. He wants to make sure that she's feeling one hundred percent by Friday."

"Oh, well then, if you won't be needing me, I was on my way home when I ran into Mr. Waterman." Turning on her heel, Susan walked back to the curb and waited for the traffic to clear.

The moment she was out of earshot, Carly said, "She has about as much personality as a stump. How long has she worked for Jenna?"

"About six months. She started out as a temporary replacement when Jenna's secretary had a baby. According to Jenna, she's very efficient."

"I wonder what she and Sam Waterman were really talking about," Carly mused.

"Probably Jenna's unavailability. It's bound to cause some comment." Holt escorted Carly into the building and toward the private elevator. "Does your family usually leave the door to your living quarters unlocked?"

"I think so. Why?"

"Susan seemed surprised that she couldn't just pop in on Jenna."

The moment the elevator doors slid open, Tom

Chadwick strode out, then stopped short in front of Holt.

"You." He poked a finger into Holt's chest. "I'm going to tell you to your face what I just finished telling Calvin. If you don't trust me anymore, just ask for my resignation."

Carly edged closer to Holt. "What happened, Tom?"

Tom turned to her. "This morning your father asked me to download all of the research on the tea project I've done here in the lab onto disks. He wouldn't tell me why. And just now, when I handed the disks to him, I learned that some of the research is being done elsewhere." He whirled back to Holt. "I want to know why I wasn't informed. Isn't my work good enough? I've been with this company for more than fifteen years."

"It has nothing to do with the quality of your work," Holt said. "It was merely a matter of security."

Tom snorted as he moved past Holt. "Security! Well, there's certainly a big enough security staff around here since you came. Maybe they'd like to do part of the research, too."

"Maybe it was a mistake to leave my father alone here all day," Carly said as she watched Tom storm out of the building. "Subtle, he's not."

"He's doing exactly what he's supposed to be doing. Stirring up the waters and reinforcing the reason he can't put his hand on the research instantly," Holt explained as he guided her onto the elevator and inserted his key to the penthouse level.

When they reached the lobby, Mark Miller was stepping out of Calvin's office. His face was flushed. "I wouldn't go in there," Mark warned Carly. "He's not through with Danny yet." Then he turned to Holt.

"Should we expect more of these third-degree tactics once you're in charge?"

"Why are you so quick to blame Holt?" Carly asked. "It's my father who's been giving you a hard time."

Mark's eyebrows rose. "Your father has never accused me of having a loose tongue before. And there was never a security guard stationed at the door to your living quarters before. I naturally assumed the changes had to do with the upcoming switch in leadership after the wedding on Friday. That is, if there's still going to be a wedding."

"Of course there's going to be a wedding," Carly said. "Why would you think there isn't?"

"Guards can be used to keep people in as well as out," Mark said as he moved past them into the elevator.

"I've never seen him that angry," Carly observed as Holt hurried her down the hall to the family quarters. They were still out of the guard's earshot when Holt stopped and turned to her.

"They've never been happy with the security system I installed. Your father wasn't too keen on it, either. He's more trusting than I am. He didn't object to it when I arranged to have all of our offices randomly swept for bugs, but he drew the line when I wanted to do the same in the penthouse."

Carly studied him for a minute. "You're saying you think our apartment's bugged?"

"It's a strong possibility. Think about it. We weren't followed to Lance's building. Someone was waiting on the roof for us. They knew ahead of time where we were going."

"And someone could also have known I was going

to your apartment on Monday morning to propose to you."

"C'mon," Holt said. "We'll check Jenna's bedroom first. Don't say a word."

The moment they shut the door behind them, Holt took off his jacket and immediately began to search the room, running his hand beneath the flat surface on the nightstand. From her habitual position at the foot of the bed, Priscilla raised her head and blinked, then went back to sleep.

What the penthouse needed, Carly decided, was a pair of good watchdogs like Sir Gawain and the Green Knight. Then it might not have been so easy to plant a bug. Shrugging out of her coat, she studied what Holt was doing and then ran her hand beneath the edge of the dresser. She wasn't even sure what she was looking for. And then she saw it, the reflection of Jenna's wedding dress in the mirror above the dresser. Turning, she looked at it hanging from the closet door.

It literally took her breath away. The lace was so finely woven, and even in the artificial light it glittered. It looked like the kind of dress a fairy godmother would conjure up out of dewdrops with the wave of a wand. Fragile as a dream, it could just as easily be waved away.

Less than two days ago, she'd hopped in a cab, determined to convince Holt Cassidy to marry her. Seeing the dress made her proposal seem suddenly more real. And more unattainable.

On Monday morning, everything had seemed so simple, so clear. Everything had fit logically on a note card. She'd been so confident that she could attract him, convince him.

Now everything was complicated. He was drawing

away, and she wanted him even more. Nothing was clear except the fact that she wanted to wear that wedding dress on Friday and walk down the aisle on Holt Cassidy's arm. But her reasons had changed. She wasn't even sure she could name them all, let alone list them on a note card.

She looked at him and saw that he'd climbed onto the mattress and pulled the pillows back so that he could search the headboard. As he stretched himself across the bed, the jeans and turtleneck sweater he was wearing revealed every lean plane and angle of his body. She felt a flame flicker to life in her stomach and spread.

She could see herself on that bed, her limbs tangled with his. It was the same image that had filled her mind when he'd taken her hand and pulled her to her feet outside his building. Only now, the picture was sharper, stronger. More tempting. She felt her throat dry up, and the air grew thicker, more difficult to breathe.

He turned and gestured her closer. Neither of them said a thing. Neither of them moved. Then his eyes narrowed, willing her to come. She felt the pull. As strong and as inevitable as gravity. The bed suddenly seemed larger, the room smaller. And she was moving toward him before she could stop herself. It occurred to her that she'd never wanted anything, anyone this intensely. And it wasn't just the physical pleasure she would have with him, though she knew that would be incredible. What drew her even more was the man himself, the quietness she'd sensed in him from the beginning, the solitude. And the deep wellspring of kindness that she'd only begun to discover. She loved the man who claimed he didn't trust anyone, but who'd defended her father when she'd begun to doubt.

On Monday she'd wanted to get married. Now she wanted to marry Holt Cassidy. And she would never want to marry anyone else. That realization had fear racing through her, mixing with the desire.

Glancing at Jenna's wedding dress again, Carly suddenly remembered her plan. And she also remembered Lania's strategy. Keep close, but keep your distance. It seemed like years since she'd jotted those words down. And in her mind she could see her note card shredding into hundreds of pieces and falling like snow. If she climbed into that bed now and took what she wanted, she would risk everything, but if risking everything was what it took... She lifted her knee to the edge of the bed.

When he'd lifted his hand to signal her to come closer, Holt had wanted to show her the voice-activated tape recorder fastened beneath the slat of the headboard. The instant he'd looked at her, his intention had changed. His throat had gone dry as dust. As she walked slowly toward him, need and longing had twisted so tightly in him that he ached with it. If he'd ever seen anyone more beautiful, he couldn't remember. But he was sure that he'd never wanted anyone this intensely. She was so small, so lovely, and the mere thought of touching her made his hand tremble. He lowered it to the bed.

He'd brought her back here to leave her with her father, to rid himself of the responsibility, the temptation. He tried desperately to remember those intentions.

If she came to him now, he wouldn't resist. He couldn't. And they both knew it. The knowledge, the surety of it hung in the air between them. His heart was drumming with it. His vision was clouding.

And then he saw, reflected in the mirror, the wedding dress.

And he knew that he couldn't make love to her, not now.

He didn't want to hurt her.

It took all of his strength to lift himself off the bed. Before he could change his mind, he walked quickly into the bathroom and signaled her to follow.

Carly felt the rejection as clearly as if he'd slapped her hard. No, it was as if he'd sliced her open with a knife, she decided as she wrapped her arms around herself. For a moment she stayed right where she was with her knee still on the bed, grateful that he'd turned his back to her. She needed a minute to regain her equilibrium, to remind herself to breathe again. As she finally turned and followed him into the bathroom, she reached for logic, anything that would help soothe the hurt that had spread through her entire body.

Had she misinterpreted what he'd meant? No, there was no way she'd mistaken the look she'd seen in his eyes.

Clearly, he'd changed his mind.

And he'd saved her, hadn't he? From making a mistake? From veering from her plan? A plan she'd tossed away the moment he'd crooked a finger at her and turned her mind to mush!

What was happening to her? She'd always been able to focus on her goals and achieve them. He was changing that. Changing her. And she couldn't allow that to happen.

The moment she walked through the door, he shut it

gently behind her. He'd turned the shower on. Curious, she walked toward it and tested the water. Cold.

Turning, she faced him across three feet of tiled floor and lifted her chin. "A cold shower? Is that your remedy whenever you change your mind? It's a very primitive solution. The men on the island often have to resort to using the waterfall at the lagoon."

In a movement so quick she couldn't avoid it, he gripped her chin in his hand. "I didn't change my mind. And when we make love, a little cold water won't interfere."

He spoke the words softly, but she had no trouble hearing the threat. She had even less trouble seeing the promise in his eyes. The little band of pain around her heart eased suddenly.

Holt dropped his hand and cursed himself silently as he stepped back to lean against the sink. The words had been out before he could stop them. And he hadn't meant to touch her, either. Why was it that every time he decided to turn away, he seemed compelled to move toward her instead? Folding his arms across his chest, he said, "Right now, I'm using the shower for white noise. The bugging device I found on the headboard isn't very high-tech. The tape has to be collected and replaced periodically. The security guard might prevent that for the time being, but I don't want to take any chances, just in case someone has found other access to your apartment. I don't want to deactivate it, either. If we don't let them know we've found it, we may be able to make some use of it ourselves."

"Are you saying that someone knows everything that has been said in this room?" Carly asked.

Holt nodded. "From the day the tape recorder was planted."

"So if Jenna talked to Lance on the phone..."

"We have to assume everything was recorded." Holt studied her as she absorbed and began to process the information, and he found himself envying her ability to totally concentrate on the problem at hand. He was still thinking of her. Still wanting. He now knew that as long as he was anywhere near her, he wasn't going to be able to think clearly.

"This eliminates Lance, then," Carly said. "He wouldn't have to bug Jenna's room for information."

"No. But this also makes it more of a certainty that one of the people here at Carpenter Enterprises is behind the blackmail. C'mon." Holt reached for the door handle. "We'll check your room and your father's. And then we'll have to tell him."

CALVIN CARPENTER WAS not happy with the news. But aside from shredding one of his cigars when he learned that it was Lance Bigelow who'd eloped with Jenna, he'd taken the whole thing more calmly than Carly had thought he would. At first he'd wanted to make Lance into the villain. But Holt had slowly but surely managed to talk him out of that scenario, using logic and the evidence they'd uncovered. Only Jenna's room had been bugged. If Lance had managed to make her fall in love with him again, he wouldn't have had to plant a recording device in her room. He could have gotten any information he needed from Jenna.

Leaning forward, Calvin folded his arms on the desk and glanced at Carly, then back at Holt. "So it turns out my little girl here was right. Jenna's elopement with Lance Bigelow is just something that this damn blackmailer is taking advantage of because he wants to get his hands on the formula for Carly's tea project?"

"It's the only theory that seems to explain everything that's been happening," Holt said. "First, someone finds out that Jenna, who is engaged to marry me, is seeing someone else. Perhaps because of the bug. Or perhaps the room was bugged after the affair was discovered. But one way or the other, this person, the blackmailer, learns about the elopement and sees an opportunity to use it to extort the formula from you. The plan seems simple, risk-free, because the person believes that with the wedding about to take place, you'll act quickly to get your daughter back. And by the time the hoax is discovered, he and his partner will have the formula and the research."

"Then Carly arrives for the wedding and throws a wrench into the works by proposing to you," Calvin continued. "Without the pressure of having to call the wedding off, I can stall for time. Which I do."

"And each day that goes by increases the risk of us finding out that Jenna has really eloped. Which we have," Carly said. "So the blackmailer is starting to panic."

"And the person who poses the biggest threat to the plan is Carly," Holt said. "Carly has to be scared off, or eliminated, so that the Carpenter–Cassidy wedding can't take place on Friday. Therefore, in order to protect Carly, we have to call off the wedding."

He'd said the words so calmly that Carly was sure she'd misunderstood him at first. Calvin, too, was silent for a moment as the words slowly sank in. Then the older man erupted from his chair. "What are you talking about?"

Holt remained seated. His voice was calm when he spoke. "If we announce that the wedding is off, then no one will be worried that Carly is going to stand in for her sister. She'll no longer pose a threat to anyone."

Planting his palms flat on his desk, Calvin leaned toward the younger man. "Now, wait just a minute. You signed an agreement. Marrying my daughter was a part of it."

Holt rose and moved to the desk. "You know as well as I do how that agreement reads. It has Jenna's name on it, and it states clearly that she has to be willing to marry me. The elopement relieves me of any legal obligation to—"

Calvin interrupted him with a short expletive. "You're talking about the letter of the law. I'm talking about the spirit of that agreement we signed. We'll see which one of us prevails in court."

"I'm talking about your daughter's safety. I want her out of this!"

Hurrying forward, Carly slapped her hands down on the desk to get their attention. "I'm not getting out of this. And I'm tired of being discussed as if I weren't in the room. I've been running my life on my own for quite a while now, and I'm perfectly capable of deciding what to do without help from either one of you."

"Carly—" Holt began.

"Now, just a minute, little girl—"

Carly whirled on her father. "I'm *not* a little girl." Then she turned to Holt. "And the legalities of the contract you signed with my father are irrelevant right now. You can't cancel the wedding because it's the only pressure the blackmailer has. Take it away from him and you could force him to do something we'll all regret."

"I want you safe," Holt said.

Walking around the edge of the desk, Carly stood

toe to toe with him. "I want my sister safe. There's a recording device in her room, for heaven's sake. What if the blackmailer knows where she and Lance have gone on their honeymoon? What if he can put his hand on her anytime he wants? We can't afford to cancel the wedding until we know for sure she's safe."

"She's right," Calvin said with a hint of pride in his voice. "Smart girl."

"All right." Holt didn't take his eyes from Carly. "But until we find out who's behind this, you're not leaving this penthouse." He turned to Calvin. "And you're going to see to it that she stays here."

Whatever Calvin would have replied was cut off by the ringing of the phone. Moving to the desk, he punched the speaker button. Immediately, the distorted, metallic-sounding voice poured into the room.

"You have until tomorrow at noon to get the research ready or you won't see Jenna again. Fax in transit."

Just as the dial tone sounded, the fax machine on the credenza behind Calvin's desk began to hum. Holt and Carly hurried to join Calvin as the paper rolled out of the machine.

The picture was grainy, but Carly could easily identify Jenna, and even though it had been nine years, she recognized Lance, too. The photographer had captured them laughing, and Lance was holding a pair of skis in his hand.

"They do know where Lance and Jenna are," Carly whispered. "We've got to find out where they went on their honeymoon. It looks like a ski resort. We've got to warn them."

Holt took her hands in his. "Lance isn't due to call his office until Friday. He probably realized that we'd try to trace him that way, and he didn't want to risk it until the wedding was over. But Molly Lieberman said she dropped them off at the airport. I'll have one of the security people go over the flight rosters again."

"Have them look for names from the King Arthur legend," Carly suggested. "Better still, bring the rosters here, and we'll look them over."

"Right," Holt agreed.

"And the restaurants they were meeting at," Carly said as she started toward the door. "We have to check them out."

"No way. You're not taking a step out of this building until we can be sure that no one is out there waiting to drop a rock on your head. I'll go. Where are the matches?"

"In the bottom drawer of Jenna's dresser."

"I'll do the field research on my own this time," Holt said.

Carly wanted to reach out to him as he walked past her. But she knew it wouldn't do any good. And she knew, as the door closed behind him, that he was going to walk out of her life as surely as he was leaving the office. It had hurt when he'd gotten up off the bed earlier. But now she felt numb. Finally she turned back to her father.

"Don't blame you a bit, little girl. I'd like to be doing more myself." Reaching into his desk drawer, he pulled out a bottle of brandy and poured two glasses.

As Carly walked toward her father, she noticed for the first time how tired he looked. Older and more fragile, too. She thought about the strain he'd been under. A company he'd spent his whole life building was being threatened, probably by someone he'd trusted. One of his daughters was missing, and the other was dodging speeding cars and falling bricks. When he handed her the glass, she took a long swallow and then said the thing that was foremost in her mind. "He's going to cancel the wedding. Just as soon as we get Jenna back."

Calvin sat down in his chair and studied his daughter. "You could change his mind."

"No." She took another sip of her drink and settled her hip on the corner of his desk. "He doesn't want to marry me. I thought I could convince him. I was so sure.... First I tried logic. Then I tried to attract him, make him want me. I thought I knew a lot about it. It's what I've been studying for the past two years. Dating rituals. Girl meets boy. Girl gets boy. It looks great on note cards." She set her glass down with a sigh. "But it's not working."

"Holt doesn't want to marry anyone, your sister included. I didn't think I'd ever get him to agree to that contract." Leaning back, Calvin sipped his brandy, but he kept his eyes steady on his daughter. "Holt Cassidy gives new meaning to the word *loner*. He didn't even want to come to work for me. I had a devil of a time convincing him. He just wanted me to invest in a company he could run by himself."

"He doesn't trust anyone."

"No, he doesn't. First thing he did when he came here was to run a background check on everyone who works here. He keeps the files in his office." Calvin took another drink of his brandy. "Never trust anyone. He learned that lesson the hard way when he was a kid. Not that he'll ever talk about it. But I ran a background check on him, too."

Carly ran her finger around the rim of her glass. "Jenna told me he lost his parents when he was only four. And then he went through a series of foster homes until he ran away to join the merchant marine."

"It was the first foster home he stayed in that killed his ability to trust people. They kept him there for two years and they were in the process of adopting him when the woman he'd come to accept and love as his mother became pregnant. Instead of going through with the adoption, they sent him back into the foster care system. They were having their own child, so they didn't want him anymore."

Carly stared at her father. "Then he lost his family twice. I can't even imagine... It was hard enough losing Mom, but I was fifteen. He must have been...what? Six?" Rising, she paced over to the window and looked out at the darkness. Snow had begun to fall, and the lights of the city were blurred. She felt helpless.

"He needs a home and a family of his own, little girl."

Turning, she faced her father. "I don't know what to do."

Calvin walked to his daughter and laid a hand along her cheek. "I can count the times on one hand that you've asked me for advice. Even when you were little, you were so independent. Your mother said you were like me." He hesitated for a moment and then dropped his hand. "I want to give you the right answer, but I think you'll have to find your own."

When she said nothing but merely continued to look at him, Calvin searched for the appropriate words. "I can tell you how I convinced your mother." He winced slightly. "Came damned close to losing her before I figured it out."

Carly's lips curved. "That's hard to imagine. I always figured you just swept her off her feet and carried her off."

"Yeah, I did that, all right." Calvin smiled at a memory only he could see. "But it turned out to be a mistake."

Intrigued, Carly studied him closely. "I didn't think Calvin Carpenter made mistakes."

"I don't," he said. "Usually. But your mother had a way of making me feel like a bumbling fool. She was dating Sam Waterman at the time, so jealousy could have had something to do with it. He was everything that I wasn't. A gentleman from an old family. He had money, looks, charm. I was struggling to get Carpenter Enterprises on its feet. So I did what I thought would work. I seduced her. I figured once I made love to her, she'd be mine forever."

Carly bit back a laugh. "Don't tell me she wasn't impressed?"

Calvin's chuckle was wry. "I thought she was. But I didn't get the results I expected. She stopped dating Sam. But she wouldn't go out with me, either."

"So what did you do?" Carly asked.

"I said the three hardest words in the English language. I said, 'I love you.'"

Carly considered that for a moment as a little bubble of panic formed in her stomach. "If I tell him, he could still walk away."

"That's the risk. It's the greatest one you'll ever take."

When she finally nodded, Calvin let out the breath he'd been holding. "You better go after him before you lose your courage."

Carly's eyes widened. "You mean you're going to let me—"

Calvin turned and walked to his desk. "Thanks to Holt, I've got security people seeping out of the walls mumbling to each other on walkie-talkies. I might as well put some of them to work earning an honest day's pay. I've got one of them tailing him right now." He punched a few numbers on his phone. "I'll send another one along with you."

8

BISTRO 720 WAS FILLED with the hum of conversation and bursts of laughter. Holt sat alone in a corner booth near a window. He found the bluesy jazz pouring out of a jukebox relaxing after the deafening din at Club Metro. The bartender at the popular dance club claimed he was new on the job. Not even a twenty-dollar bill had jarred his memory when Holt had shown him a picture of Jenna. So far, Carly's theory of the importance of doing fieldwork in person was a bust.

He had to admit that Bistro 720 had *some* potential. The lighting was better, for one thing. It glinted off the mahogany bar and spilled into the corners, and he could actually see the other customers. If Carly was here, she'd find the quaint neighborhood bar interesting. He could imagine the way her eyes would light up as she studied the people. They were all native New Yorkers, not a tourist in sight.

"Can I get you another beer while you're waiting?" A short woman with graying hair and a friendly smile was clearing empty glasses from a nearby table. She'd been behind the bar when he'd come in.

"I'm not waiting for anyone," Holt told her.

"A wild guess," the woman said with a shrug. "I figure a good-looking guy like you who nurses a beer for half an hour must be meeting someone. Wave when you want a refill."

Holt watched her carry her tray back behind the bar. Then he frowned at his half-empty glass. Had he been sitting here that long? Probably. And he'd just let a woman who might recognize Jenna's picture walk away from him. Oh, he could tell himself that he was waiting, hoping to establish a friendly rapport before he began to grill her about Jenna and Lance. But the truth was, he'd simply been thinking of Carly and what it might be like to have her here with him.

He missed her. She was definitely getting to him.

Lifting his glass, he took a long swallow. The beer was flat and warm. He set it back down on the table.

Careful. That had always been his watchword. He'd prided himself on that. Risks were to be taken, but only after weighing the consequences. Turning, he stared out the window. The street gleamed with the icy rain that had begun to fall.

There wasn't enough beer in the world to rid his mind of the image of Carly crossing the bedroom toward him and placing her knee on the edge of the mattress. For a moment his mind had been wiped clean. And then it had filled with her. Only her.

Even now, he wasn't sure how he'd managed to stand up and walk away. But he was certain it was more than desire he'd felt. What he felt for Carly went much deeper. It was primal. Inevitable.

He'd spent enough time on the sea, being tossed around at the mercy of the elements, to believe in fate. Perhaps it was time he stopped fighting it.

There'd be a price to pay. It might cost him everything he'd ever hoped to achieve at Carpenter Enterprises. As a child, he'd lost his whole world twice, and he'd vowed that he would never allow that to happen again.

Through the window, he saw a taxi pull to the curb. When Carly climbed out of it, he thought for a moment that he'd conjured her up. Fate. It was in that instant that he made his decision. He was going to have her. And whatever the price, he'd pay it.

"YOU'RE SURE THIS IS the place, Bob?" Carly asked as the security man helped her out of the taxi.

"Bistro 720." He pointed to the freshly painted sign on the door. "And that's Harry's car parked across the street."

Carly glanced at the dark sedan trying hard to blend in with the other cars on the street. She turned her attention back to Bistro 720. It was hard to picture the Jenna she knew at this nondescript bar. The awning overhead was frayed, and the stores flanking it on either side were shielded by padlocked iron gates.

"Ma'am, why don't you go on and join Mr. Cassidy," Bob suggested. "I'll check in with Harry."

Carly walked down the short flight of steps to the front door of the bar. She could hear laughter and music, blues with lots of deep brass. But she didn't reach for the knob. First she needed a moment to gather her thoughts and review her strategy. *Review her strategy!* Who was she kidding? There wasn't a strategy in the world that was going to help her tell a man, who didn't want to marry her if he could possibly help it, that she loved him.

She must be crazy! She was definitely in love! Shakespeare had been right on the money to call it moon madness. And there was no turning back. If she tried to run away, Bob and Harry, the security duo, would be right on her tail. Taking a deep breath, she pushed away the bubble of panic that was welling up in her. She'd dressed for success. At least she had that to hold on to. A good costume always helped. Actors swore by them. And she'd wasted twenty minutes selecting hers.

The night that Lania had finally declared her love for Lu, the night everyone on the island had celebrated their formal engagement, Lania had worn white. Carly could still picture her with flowers in her hair, the filmy material of her dress billowing in the soft ocean breeze.

But this was winter in Manhattan, and she didn't want her teeth to chatter in the middle of her declaration. So she'd settled for ivory leggings and a matching V-necked sweater. The flowers were out, too. One of them would probably fall out of her hair and bop her in the nose just as she said those three little words.

I love you. Before the words could form a chant in her head and paralyze her legs, she reached for the door handle and gripped it hard. She could do this. Millions of women before her had done this. It must have worked. Otherwise, the human race would now be extinct. Pulling the door open, she walked into the bar.

The moment she saw Holt sitting alone in the booth, some of her tension eased. But as she drew closer, the look in his eyes had it building all over again. By the time she reached him, her mouth felt parched. It was Holt who spoke first.

"Of all the gin joints in the world..."

Carly smiled. "A joke. I got it this time."

"My delivery must be improving."

Shrugging out of her coat, she slid into the seat across from him. "I thought you'd be furious. But this was my father's idea. He sent me with Bob, one of your security people. He'll be in, just as soon as he finishes talking to Harry. Harry, by the way, is tailing *you*."

"Your father's idea?" Holt asked.

"When I left the penthouse, he was muttering something about overpaid, underworked, so-called security people starting to earn their keep." Folding her hands, she faced Holt across the table. "I forget whose turn it is to call the shots."

"Be my guest. I struck out at Club Metro."

"You should have taken your partner."

"I should have taken earmuffs and a flashlight."

While Holt was filling her in on the dead end he'd run into at the dance club, Carly took a moment to study him. He was tired. But he was also oddly relaxed. More relaxed than she'd ever seen him. Before she had time to try to figure out why, the waitress appeared at their table.

"If you weren't waiting for this young lady, you're a very lucky man," she said to Holt. "Can I refill that beer now?"

"The lady is going to order for both of us."

The gleam of amusement in his eyes was so appealing that Carly couldn't argue. "Do you have cappuccino?" she asked the waitress.

"Absolutely. My daughter goes to NYU so she makes sure I have all the trendiest stuff. This place used to be Patsy's Pub. I kind of liked having my name on the door. But she tells me bistros are in. Two cappuccinos?"

Carly glanced at Holt.

"Still your turn," he said.

Carly wrinkled her nose at him before she turned back to the waitress. "The gentlemen would prefer tea. Herbal if you have one."

"We have a complete line of Carpenter Teas, at the request of one of my customers," Patsy informed her with a smile. "Which flavor does he prefer?"

"Something that smells like a meadow," Carly replied.

"Spring Delight," the woman murmured as she turned away.

The moment Patsy was out of earshot, Carly leaned toward Holt. "They carry Carpenter Teas. Don't you think that's odd?"

"I think it's smart," Holt said.

"But this place..." Carly paused to glance around. "They're not making their money catering to people who drink herbal teas. I think it means Jenna's been here."

"We're already pretty sure of that much." Holt reached across the table to run his finger down her earring. "You always wear the same ones. Why?"

Carly thought fast. She could hardly tell him that she hadn't taken them off since he'd touched them. "I feel lucky when I wear them."

Leaning back in the booth, Holt continued to regard her steadily. "How did you survive on that island without an espresso machine?"

There was definitely something different about him, Carly decided. It wasn't merely that he was relaxed. His eyes were different, too. Not so shuttered. She could see amusement and just a hint of the rashness she'd glimpsed in the instant before he'd kissed her that first time. She felt something skip up her spine just as her thoughts began to scatter. Quickly she made herself focus. "I took a huge supply of instant coffee along. And the island wasn't totally out of reach of civilization. Once a week a boat came over from the closest island. Manilai is still relatively isolated, though, because it's so small. And it's off the beaten path for tourists. Dr. Antolini did his original study there more than forty years ago. His purpose in going back was to see how much the culture had been affected by the island's diminishing isolation." She paused, then frowned. "I must be boring you."

Holt shook his head. "Not at all. What exactly was the focus of your study?"

"I was looking at the dating patterns, courting rituals, that sort of thing."

"Really? How did you go about it?" he asked.

"Interviews, case histories, observation. Fieldwork is pretty dull."

"You probably didn't have a partner. I suppose you took notes?"

Carly's eyes narrowed. "Tons of them." She saw his lips twitch. "What's so funny?"

"I'm picturing you following some hapless couple around on a date, scribbling notes. Didn't there come a time when they told you to back off?"

"It wasn't like that. Well, not usually. You make it sound like I was the odd man out." Which was exactly what it had felt like at times. No wonder she had come back to the States crazed to get married. She lifted her chin. "It wasn't a Masters and Johnson sex study. I merely attempted to record the way the young people in this particular village would select a mate and eventually marry."

"In other words, you've become an expert on seduction," Holt said.

She wasn't sure when he had taken her hand, but her fingers were twined with his. And she couldn't have looked away from his eyes if her life depended on it.

What she saw in them made her heart start to hammer. She'd seen that look before. In the eyes of that python she'd adopted—just before he'd gobble up his prey.

All this time, she'd been so focused on pursuing Holt that she hadn't even thought of what she'd do if he turned the tables and started to pursue her. Desperately she searched for something she could say to distract him. To distract herself.

Patsy chose that moment to deliver their drinks.

"Jenna," Carly said. She didn't know how she managed to say the name, but it was enough to free her gaze from Holt's. She turned to the woman. "We're looking for my sister, Jenna. She used to come here, and she's disappeared."

"My brother's a cop," Patsy said. "The tall, skinny guy at the end of the bar. Wait, I'll—"

"No." Carly grabbed her hand. "We can't tell the police. My father got a ransom note. She could be in danger. But we really think she's eloped. We just have to find her."

Patsy studied Carly for a minute. "Let me get this straight. You think your sister has eloped, but maybe she's been kidnapped, too?"

"I know it sounds like a made-for-TV movie, but it's really happened. My father is frantic. His health isn't the best."

As she continued to explain the situation, Holt drew a picture of Jenna out of his pocket and placed it faceup on the table.

Patsy glanced down at it and then back at Carly. "You look like your sister."

"Then you've seen her?" Carly slid over in the booth to make room for the woman.

"Sure, she's been a regular here for maybe five, six

months. Every Tuesday night, except for last night, she
meets this nice-looking guy. They usually sit right here
in this booth."

"Did they talk to anyone, any of your regular customers?" Holt asked. "We have to find out where
they've gone."

Patsy shook her head, frowning. "They always kept
to themselves. In fact, I got the impression that they
wanted to keep their meetings a secret. Sometimes, he
would arrive first. Other times, she would. I thought
maybe one of them was married. They were even followed once."

"Who followed them?" Carly asked.

"A woman. She came in and sat in the booth right
next to theirs, drank white wine and read a book. We
don't get a lot of strangers in here midweek. I still
might not have thought anything about it, but when
your sister and her gentleman friend left, this woman
was very interested in their booth. That's when I
thought maybe this woman was a P.I. She was about to
sit down in the booth when I went over to clear it. She
paid her bill and left in a hurry then."

"She might have been thinking about planting a
bug," Holt said. "What did she look like?"

Patsy frowned thoughtfully. "Kind of medium
height. She had brown hair, wore a hat, a sort of beret.
To tell you the truth, she's someone who doesn't stand
out in your mind. That's why I thought she was a P.I.
But then I do watch a lot of TV." Suddenly Patsy's expression brightened. "You know, that was the night
my daughter found something on the floor under this
booth when she was sweeping up. I'd forgotten all
about it. It was a travel brochure for a ski lodge in Vermont or New Hampshire, the one that's run by the von

Trapp family—you know, from *The Sound of Music*. I tossed it out, but I remember the name because of the movie. But that's all I remember."

"Thank you so much," Carly said. "You've been a big help." She could hardly wait for Patsy to get out of earshot before she leaned toward Holt. "That's it. Carly and Lance have gone to the Trapp Family Lodge. I know it."

"Carly," Holt said, "a travel brochure swept up in the general vicinity of the booth your sister and Lance sat in is not exactly conclusive evidence."

"They were holding skis in that picture the kidnappers faxed."

"True. But there are a lot of ski resorts."

"That's just the point. Of all the ski resorts in all the world, this is the one that Jenna would choose. For months after Lance and his family disappeared, she played the soundtrack of *Camelot* over and over and *over*. I knew she was getting better when she switched to *The Sound of Music*. That was when she decided to become a nun, but at least she was making progress."

"I still don't see why you're so sure—"

"When Guinevere and Lancelot tried to run away, they got caught. When Captain von Trapp and Maria tried to escape from the Nazis, they succeeded. Eventually they came to this country and built a ski lodge. Trust me. Jenna and Lance are honeymooning at their ski resort!"

Holt studied her for a minute, then pulled out his cellular phone. "I suppose it's worth checking."

For the next several minutes, while Holt was busy issuing orders over his cell phone, Carly downed her cappuccino and shredded the paper napkin it had been sitting on. The initial sense of relief and excitement that had flooded through her because she knew where her sister was, had faded. In its place was all the apprehension and fear that had been bubbling up in her when she'd first arrived at the bar. Any minute now, Holt would finish arranging for someone to go to the Trapp family ski resort, and she would have to do what she'd come here to do.

Just then Holt reached over and took her hand. "I don't want you to be too hopeful. This could be a wild-goose chase."

She couldn't have agreed with him more. And not about finding Jenna. She watched him signal Patsy for the bill. When he turned back to her, she knew it was now or never.

"Before we go, there's something I want to tell you," she said. "I love you."

His hand tightened almost painfully on hers, and she saw something in his eyes, something...and then nothing. Her father had promised that saying the words would free her. But instead she felt trapped in the endless swirl of fog that she now saw in his eyes.

Patsy's voice seemed to come from a distance. "You ready for the check?"

"I'll have a martini," Holt said.

Carly's eyes widened, but she felt a little bud of hope begin to bloom inside her. "Make that two."

Holt spoke the moment Patsy walked away. "You don't drink martinis."

"I didn't think you did, either, Mr. Spring-Delight-Vegetarian-Special-Pizza. And don't tell me they're good for you just because they come with an olive in them."

Holt released her hand and leaned back in the booth. "Every time I come up with a plan to handle you, you do something that changes everything. You are the most exasperating woman."

Carly's chin lifted. "Yeah, well, you're not the easiest person to deal with, either. I screw up my courage, track you down in your apartment at the crack of dawn to propose, an offer that my sister assures me you'll snap right up, and you don't even bother to give me an answer. Now I tell you I love you, and you order a drink."

"I need a drink," Holt said.

"Me, too."

Neither one of them spoke again until the martinis arrived. Then Carly drained half of hers. It burned her throat a little, but then the warmth began to move slowly through her. Leaning back, she studied Holt. "You're angry."

"No—" Holt stopped himself. It was a lie. He was angry, and that was easier to deal with than the other emotions her words had set loose in him. He couldn't sort through them all, but he recognized one of them as fear. He took a sip of his own drink. "I'm angry at this whole situation." That was true enough. "You don't really want to marry me, Carly. You're doing it for your family. You love them. You'd do anything to clear up this mess that your sister left behind by running off with Lance."

Carly drained the rest of her drink. "That's not true. I'm a big girl. I fought very hard for my independence, and I don't do anything I don't want to do. My father may have advised me to tell you that I love you, but I meant it, and I'm prepared to take the consef-ences...consequences."

"There, you see. Your father advises you to tell me you love me. He'll do anything he can to make sure

that I marry one of his daughters on Friday. Now that
Jenna's eloped, that leaves you. He wants to make sure
that his grandchildren have a future in the company he
founded."

"Phooey," Carly said, reaching for his drink. "You
don't really want that, do you?" She managed one sip
before he removed his glass from her hand. "I may
have proposed to you because of my family. But I
didn't tell you I love you because of them. I have my
own reasons for wanting to marry you. I had them
listed on a note card, but it's back at the penthouse, and
I'm not sure I can remember them." She paused to
press her hands to her temples. It seemed to be right
there that her thoughts were trying to escape. The moment they settled, she continued. "I don't love you because of my family. And it has nothing to do with your
being King Arthur. You're not anything like him. Well,
I suppose Carpenter Enterprises is a little like Camelot." She paused to wave a hand. "That is, if you really
want to stretch it. But if my father is supposed to be
Merlin, he's really having a bad magic day!"

"Carly, I think we should—"

"No. I have to finish this. It's very important. Wait a
minute." She moved her fingers to the center of her
forehead and held them there to make sure the thought
didn't escape. Then she tried hard to remember what
she wanted to say. "I never really could see why Guinevere ran off with Lancelot anyway. So he was the
great romantic knight on horseback. Big deal. I would
have chosen Arthur over him any day because he had
such goodness, such a vision for his kingdom." Suddenly she was very tired. She could feel her eyes closing. "Besides, he was sexy as hell." There. She could

sleep now. And putting her head down on her arms, that's just what she did.

HOLT STARED into the darkness outside the window of his apartment. Any light seeping into the early morning sky was masked by the steadily falling snow. It occurred to him that Manhattan had seen more snow in the past few days than it normally saw in a season. If he was superstitious, he might believe that Carly had brought the storms with her. She was undeniably the cause of the storm that was raging within him.

Turning, he looked at her sleeping on the rug in front of his fireplace. She hadn't moved since he'd put her there almost five hours ago. And he hadn't stopped watching her.

His reasons for bringing her to his apartment had been purely practical. Keeping her with him freed up one half of the Bob and Harry security duo to go to Vermont and check out the Trapp Family Lodge. When he'd told Calvin what he was doing, the old man had agreed. Carly couldn't be trusted to stay put at the Carpenter Building. Until they were sure that Jenna and Lance were safe, Holt didn't intend to let Carly out of his sight.

But he'd known the moment he carried her into his living room that he'd made a mistake. He hadn't put her in his bed. He hadn't dared to even carry her into his bedroom. If he had, he wouldn't have left. And she wouldn't have slept alone. Instead, he'd lain her on the fur rug and tucked a blanket around her. Then he'd built a fire and stood watch. Like a knight of old, guarding his lady.

The Arthurian legend had slipped into his mind more than once during the night. It might be a fantasy, but it was easier to think about and much easier to dismiss than the battle he'd been waging within himself from the moment he'd met her. Moving to the fireplace, he pulled out the screen and quietly added a log. Then he turned to study her, watching as the light from the flames danced on her face.

He couldn't figure her out. In sleep she looked so fragile, defenseless. Her collarbone and the tiny bones in her wrist were almost delicate. And her skin had the pale, translucent look of fine porcelain. But he'd experienced firsthand the power beneath that frail appearance. He thought of the way she'd attacked that punching bag at the health club. More than once, he'd seen her go toe to toe with her father. And he'd felt her turn to thunder and lightning in his arms.

As he watched the firelight flicker over her skin, he recalled picturing her just this way in his mind. But it wasn't desire he was feeling right now, nor was it the primal lust she could arouse in him so quickly. No, this was different. What he wanted more than anything else was to protect her. Cherish her.

Suddenly uncomfortable, he rose. Carly wouldn't want a man to defend her. She'd fight her own battles. She wouldn't want a knight to carry her off. His lips curved. She probably wouldn't even get on the poor guy's horse. Or if she did, she'd put all of her energy into wiggling off. No, she'd demand equal footing with any man. She'd insist on being his partner. Carly Carpenter would make a true consort for a king.

The idea wiped the smile from his face. Needing some distance, he walked back to the window. It was a ridiculous thought. A fantasy he couldn't afford to indulge in. Staring out at the snow, he rubbed his hands over his face. He hadn't been thinking straight since she'd said that four-letter word. *Love*. And seeing her here, in his apartment, had only made it worse. He didn't want love. Why in the world would he want to mess up his life with something that never lasted— something that always hurt? But as the night had slowly worked its way toward dawn, he'd felt his will weakening, his need growing.

And if she did love him...? No, he wouldn't let himself think about it. The attraction between them was so strong she was confusing it with love.

She couldn't be in love with him. It was that fierce loyalty she had to her family. She'd do anything to protect them. What she really needed was someone to protect her from herself.

He tried to ignore the question pushing at the back of his mind. *Who was going to protect him?*

CARLY WOKE SLOWLY, as she usually did, with one sensation at a time creeping into her consciousness. It was the sound of the fire she was aware of first—the soft fall of a log, the hiss of a flame, followed by the flickering of light beyond her eyelids, and finally the heat.

Opening her eyes, she recognized the crossed swords over the mantel. Holt's apartment. Suddenly all that had happened at Bistro 720 poured into her mind. She'd fallen asleep, right after telling Holt that she loved him. She shouldn't have had that martini. Or maybe her subconscious mind had provided her with an escape from the humiliation of his reaction. Or lack of it.

Either way, she'd blown it big-time. What in the world was she going to do now?

Turning, she could just make him out in the shadows. Alone, standing on the sidelines. And that's where he would always prefer to be. A little band of pain tightened around her heart.

Was it any wonder that her father's advice had failed? Love was something that would terrify Holt. When he was a child, it had been snatched away from him not once, but twice. When her father had said those words to her mother, they'd meant something. But the words meant nothing to Holt. So she wouldn't use them again. Not until he was ready to hear them.

But he shouldn't be alone. Rising, she walked toward him. Without a strategy, without a note card, without even so much as a clue to what she was going to say or do. Lania would never have made this kind of uncalculated move. She was much too smart. But Manhattan was a different kind of island. And Carly knew as she reached Holt and looked into his eyes, that she had nothing left to lose. She'd already lost her heart.

"There's no word on Jenna yet," Holt said.

For just a second, Carly was appalled. Jenna hadn't been on her mind even once since she'd woken up. All she'd thought of was Holt. Besotted, that's what she was. She dragged her thoughts back to what Holt was saying.

"No one by the name of Bigelow or Carpenter is registered at the resort. As soon as the day shift comes on, Bob is going to see if someone can identify their pictures."

"They'll be there," Carly said. She was sure of it. "I know Jenna. I've even forgotten to worry about her. Does Dad know?"

Holt nodded. "I told him I sent Bob up there to check it out when I informed him where you were spending the night."

"Right." Carly winced slightly. Then she cleared her throat. "About last night. I don't usually—"

"Why don't we forget about last night?"

"Oh. Sure." Carly managed a smile.

"While we're waiting to hear about the honeymooners, I can offer you breakfast." Turning, Holt started toward the kitchen. He'd seen the brief wounded look in her eyes. He knew that he'd never forget the words she'd spoken, but it would be better for both of them if she did. It would be better for both of them if he walked away.

"Wait."

One word. That's all it took to make him turn back. In the pale light that was just beginning to filter through the window, she looked like a goddess that one of her primitive tribes might worship. An enchantress.

"Making breakfast isn't the only thing we could do to pass the time," she said, walking toward him. "Can you remember whose turn it is to make the call? Should we make breakfast or make love? Tell you what. Since you don't have any coffee…"

He had only to look in her eyes to see what she was feeling, the desire that so clearly echoed his own. And the challenge that had need arrowing through him. How could he want her so fiercely and still want to smile? To laugh with the joy of it? "Carly, you don't know what you're doing."

She smiled. "You've got that right. I haven't a clue. My research never went this far. But you can tell me what you want. I'm a very quick learner." Taking his hands, she drew him with her toward the fire. "This is definitely your call."

Holt couldn't have said whether it was a request or a

command. All he knew was that he didn't have the power to refuse her. Any warnings still lingering in his mind slipped away. His desire to protect her, to protect himself vanished. Right now there was only Carly. "Take your clothes off," he said.

Slowly, she slipped the sweater over her head. Then, just as slowly, she pushed the leggings down one leg, then the other, and stepped free of them.

He said nothing as he stared at her. He'd pictured her like this in his mind, with the firelight flickering softly over her skin. He would remember her this way always. More than anything he wanted to touch her. Instead, he simply looked and looked until she trembled.

Her skin was paler, even creamier than the thin scrap of silk and lace she still wore. Her waist was so narrow, her legs slender as a wish and longer than he'd dreamed.

Her hand was shaking when she slipped her fingers beneath the strap of her bra to slide it off her shoulder.

His voice wasn't steady when he said, "No. Come here." When she reached him, he said, "Touch me."

"I will," she promised as she raised her hands to frame his face. "But I want you to know that this has nothing to do with my family or Carpenter Enterprises. I choose to do this because I want you. Only you."

He felt a streak of power, sharp and clean. The words were far more seducing than her scent, or even the pleasure her hands promised as she ran them down his chest to slip beneath his sweater. Even more than her touch, the words battered at him, destroying his control. Already she was making him long for something he couldn't have.

When his mouth came down on hers, it was just like

the first kiss they'd shared, hard and devouring. His lips didn't tease, his tongue didn't test. He simply demanded, and she gave. She tasted his urgency and wanted more. Craved more.

Together, they struggled to pull off his sweater and tossed it aside as they sank to their knees on the fur rug. The moment his back was bare, she ran her hands up it.

"I've wanted to do this ever since I first saw you," she said.

"I've wanted to do this." He drew her down on the rug and covered her body with his.

"Crazy," she murmured, arching beneath him as he rained kisses over her face.

"Insane," he agreed, and once more began to feast on her mouth. Slowly, inexorably, he explored her with his hands, savoring the texture of skin and then silk, and the heat his touch could leave behind. His fingers stroked, pressed, then stroked again, over her waist, down the smooth curve of her hip, up the taut muscle of her inner thigh.

More. She wasn't sure she'd said the word. She wasn't even sure her lips could form it. Or that it could be heard in this airless world he'd suddenly tossed her into.

His hands and mouth seemed to anticipate her every wish, her every dream. And still he seemed determined to show her more. She'd trained her mind to record details, but there were so many sensations. They pounded through her so quickly. How could she have lived without them before? How would she survive them now? She struggled to focus. She wanted to remember them always.

The impossible softness of the rug at her back, the

hardness in the length of his thigh, the angle of his hip. At each and every contact point, arrows of heat raced to her core, then exploded into a fire that threatened to burst out and consume them both.

She wanted him. Desperate, she tightened her arms around him and savored the fast beat of his heart, the hurried hitch of his breath, the roughness of his hands as they gripped and pressed, the quick, dizzying nip of his teeth. And the desperate sound of his voice as he whispered her name.

Everywhere he touched, she was waiting, willing. He'd never known such generosity before. Still, it wasn't enough. It would never be enough.

He wanted more. The word became a drumbeat in his head, pushing him. If he'd wanted to be gentle, he suddenly forgot as desperation roared through him. The violence of his need matched her own and her hands joined his to tug at the snap of his jeans. Together, they pulled the last barrier down over his hips and legs.

"I want you." They spoke the words together as hands sought hands, fingers linked together. *Only you.* On the wish, their eyes met and held.

This was true madness, he thought as he drove himself into her. And then he couldn't think at all. Pleasure, ecstasy...there wasn't a word to describe what he felt as she raced with him, matching him move for move, heartbeat for heartbeat. And when they reached the edge, his cry echoed hers, and they soared over it together.

For a long time neither of them moved. Holt lay very still, his head on her chest, waiting for his system to level. She'd made him lose control. And then he'd lost even more. Some vital part of himself had slipped away.

The apartment was so quiet he could hear the beat of her heart beneath his ear, the sound of her breath each time she exhaled. He didn't want to move. He could have lain right where he was forever. A log shifted in the grate, then settled.

Finally, Holt found the strength to raise his head and look at her. Her eyes were still closed, but her lips were curved with the faintest of smiles.

"Nice call," she said.

He didn't think he had the energy to laugh, but he did, rolling and shifting her so that she lay on top of him. "Perhaps you'll agree to let me make all the decisions from now on."

Folding her arms across his chest, she smiled down at him. "I don't think so. We've got this agreement. One time you make the call. The next time, I do. Remember?"

"Vaguely," he murmured as he stroked his hand down her side and then back up to settle just beneath her breast.

Her heart raced against his palm. They both felt it.

"Suppose I were to argue that what we just did was a mutual decision, and that this is my call," Holt suggested. Raising his other hand to her cheek, he drew her closer.

Unable to resist, Carly brushed her lips against his. "Arguing's against the rules. You know where it always leads."

"Let me show you," Holt said, drawing her back into a kiss.

Her mouth curved against his. "No, let me show you."

9

"ANY WORD from the Trapp Family Lodge?" Holt asked as he entered Calvin's office.

"Nothing," Calvin grumbled. "What's the point of having all these security people if they can't do their job?"

"It's early yet, barely nine o'clock. If Jenna and Lance are there, they're probably registered under an assumed name. It'll take some time to circulate their pictures and get someone to recognize them." Holt stopped at the table next to Calvin's desk and poured some tea. As he watched the pale liquid fill the mug, he found himself wishing suddenly for coffee, black and strong and hot. It had been years since he'd craved a cup of coffee.

"Well," Calvin demanded. "Are you going to stare into that cup all morning or are you going to tell me how my daughter is?"

Holt moved to the chair in front of Calvin's desk and sat down. "We'll have to wait and see. This Lance Bigelow has been very clever at covering his tracks so—"

"I'm not talking about Jenna. I'm talking about Carly."

Holt's eyebrows rose. "Carly is taking a shower. I'm sure she'll join us shortly."

Springing out of his chair, Calvin slammed a hand

down on his desk. "I'm not concerned about her personal hygiene habits. As her father, I'm concerned about the fact that she spent the night at your apartment."

Holt met Calvin's eyes squarely. "Something you no doubt anticipated when you sent her to me."

"What? Are you insinuating that I would—"

"Use your daughter to ensure the kind of future you want for Carpenter Enterprises? I don't think that's a topic that's open for debate," Holt said mildly as he set his tea down on Calvin's desk. "You talked Jenna into marrying me so that one day your grandchildren could run this company. Obviously, she wasn't happy with the arrangement. And you're not going to use Carly the same way." Rising, Holt placed his palms flat on the desk and leaned toward Calvin. "She's already done enough for this family. And for this company. Those herbs she sent back here could very well make your grandchildren millionaires. At the very least, they should buy Carly her freedom."

Calvin's eyes narrowed. "Are you telling me that you want her to go back to that island of hers and bury herself—?"

"What I'm saying is that you're not going to manipulate—"

"I'm interrupting." Carly pitched her voice to be heard above the men's arguing. When she had their attention, she closed the door and strode to the desk. "I think it's high time you both realized I make my own decisions. No one manipulates me."

Her father rounded on her. "Now, see here, little girl—"

The phone shrilled. He grabbed the receiver. "What? You're sure? They could be out on the slopes.... How long ago? Yeah...get on it." As he hung up, Calvin sank into his chair. "They're gone. Jenna and Bigelow were at the ski lodge, all right. Several people recognized the picture. But they've left. Bag and baggage. Cleaned out their room sometime during the night. Bob is trying to find someone who might have seen something."

"Maybe they just decided to leave," Carly said.

"In the middle of the night?" Calvin asked.

For a minute there was silence in the room. Then Holt said, "This time they could have really been kidnapped."

"There was no sign of a struggle," Calvin said.

"If Bigelow is behind this, there wouldn't be. Perhaps I was a little premature eliminating him as our blackmailer. But he'd have to have an accomplice. Someone who's been keeping track of our every move for the past three days. Someone who could tip him off when we were getting close, so that he could take off with Jenna."

"No." Carly began to pace. "It doesn't make sense. If Lance is behind all of this, why did someone follow Jenna and him to Bistro 720?"

"Someone followed them?" Calvin asked.

"The waitress *thought* they were being followed," Holt explained. "She could have been mistaken."

"Lance wouldn't need the listening devices we found in Jenna's bedroom, either," Carly argued.

"His accomplice might have planted it to keep track of our plans," Holt said. "In any case, I'd like to find out where Lance Bigelow has been since he disappeared from Wisconsin nine years ago. What do you know?" he asked Calvin.

The older man's eyes narrowed. "Not much. I offered his parents money, enough to make it worth their while to move away and more than enough to pay for the boy's college education. In return, they promised that he wouldn't try to contact Jenna. We all agreed it was the best solution. They were kids, much too young to be thinking of marriage."

"I hired a private detective to find Lance and his family. He couldn't come up with a trace," Carly said.

Calvin shifted uncomfortably in his chair. "I'd used that same agency you went to several times. They called me after your visit, and I paid them to tell you that."

Holt reached for the phone. "I'll have our security staff contact that agency and see what they can find out by tracing where the family went from Wisconsin. And I'll pay Lance's office another visit and see what I can dig up on his recent employment history."

"I'll go with you," Calvin offered, rising from his chair. "Bill Cavenaugh is the CEO at Sterling Securities. He and I go back—"

A knock at the door interrupted him.

"Come in," bellowed Calvin.

Susan Masterson stepped hesitantly into the room. "I was wondering if Ms. Carpenter—Jenna—is going to be in the office today?"

"No," Carly said. "The doctor is still prescribing rest."

"There's a reporter from *Nation's Business* coming at noon for an interview. Jenna's scheduled to meet with him." Susan paused, twisting her hands. "Should I cancel?"

"No, of course not. Carly will handle it," Calvin told her, waving his hands to shoo her out.

As soon as the door shut behind Susan, Carly said,

"Dad, I'm not that knowledgeable about the company."

Calvin glanced at his watch. "If Holt and I leave now, we can be back by noon. In any case, Mark Miller will be here."

"I'll go with you," Carly said. "I'll still be back in time, for the interview."

"No," Holt ordered. "You'll be safer here. I don't want anyone else dropping rocks on you."

"Holt's right, little girl," Calvin agreed. "I'm worried enough about Jenna without having to worry about you." On his way to the door, he put his arms around her and kissed her cheek. "While we're gone, why don't you consult with the executive chef downstairs and make sure we have something special for lunch? That's what your sister would do if she was here."

"Order lunch?" Carly asked in disbelief.

Holt reached for her, gripping her by the shoulders. "Think of it as your chance to escape a vegetarian pizza with sprouts." He waited until her eyes met his. "Humor me. I need your father's expertise for the fieldwork this time. We'll get back faster if we don't have to worry about you." When she still hesitated, he said, "My call."

And the next call was hers, Carly thought as she watched the door swing shut behind them. If Holt was already thinking of walking away from her, she was going to make it count.

"THIS IS JENNA'S schedule for the day?" Carly stared in disbelief at the day planner that Susan Masterson had carefully turned toward her so she could read it.

"Ms. Carpenter—Jenna—is quite organized," Susan said primly. "She writes everything down."

"Besides this interview, all she has to do is prepare menus for the executive chef?" Carly flipped over a few pages. "Is this all she usually does besides go to the gym to work out?"

"Of course not," Susan replied. "She's the vice president in charge of public relations. She has to plan parties and entertain clients from out of town. Plus, she's the company's official spokesperson. Whenever we open a store, she arranges the event and is present at the opening ceremonies. She'll be an invaluable help to Mr. Cassidy."

The perfect corporate wife, Carly thought, and kept herself from making a face. "I think I can handle planning a menu. Tell the executive chef to create some pizzas with the works. Sausage, pepperoni, not too many veggies. And he can save the sprouts for the salad."

"Certainly," Susan replied.

Susan's face was so serious that Carly made a quick escape into Jenna's office and shut the door behind her. She needed a moment to think. And not about menus. Ever since she and Holt had left his apartment, her emotions had been on a roller-coaster ride. She'd been humming a little song in her head. She'd even sung it out loud in the shower.

It was ridiculous. It was wonderful. And the song hadn't even faded when she'd heard Holt and her father yelling about sending her back to Manilai. As if they could.

Not that it didn't hurt that Holt might still want her out of his life. It did. She rubbed at the tightness that seemed to center right around her heart. But he wasn't going to call that particular shot. She wasn't going to allow it.

Moving to Jenna's desk, she ran her hand over its smooth surface. A smile curved her lips, and the little song in her head grew louder as she recalled the first time Holt kissed her. She'd wanted him so much. She'd even thought of making love to him right here on this desk.

But she didn't kid herself that making love had changed the way Holt felt about her. With a sigh, she moved to the window. Outside the snow swirled, battling the force of gravity. She could certainly sympathize with that. What had drawn her to Holt had felt as inevitable as gravity. And falling in love with him had only made the pull stronger.

But that didn't mean that Holt felt the same way. Absently, she rubbed at her heart again. She'd known that falling in love would be crazy. Now she knew that it was scary, too. What she needed was a plan. But for the first time in her life, she was absolutely clueless.

"Hi." Mark Miller stuck his head in the door. "Got a minute?"

"Sure." Carly smiled and waved him in.

"Can I bring you tea or a vitamin drink?" Susan asked from the doorway.

"Nothing for me," Mark replied.

"I don't suppose you have something with caffeine..." Carly began. When Susan's eyes widened, she quickly added, "Only joking."

The moment the secretary left the room, Carly turned to Mark. "She has absolutely no sense of humor. Why did Jenna ever hire her?"

Mark smiled. "When Miss Carter left to have her

baby six months ago, Jenna was having anxiety attacks. Miss Masterson came highly recommended."

"Well, anxiety attacks I understand," Carly said as she settled herself on the arm of a chair. "You're probably having one yourself because Jenna won't be here to handle that interview at noon."

Mark frowned. "Just how sick is your sister?"

"Now, there's a sixty-four-thousand-dollar question if I ever heard one," Tom Chadwick announced from the open doorway. Without waiting for an invitation, he strolled into the office and shut the door, settling himself in a chair next to Mark's. "Mark here believes that Jenna's skipped out on her wedding. Is he right?"

"Of course not," Carly said. "Jenna loves this company. She's worried about our father's health. Why in the world would she run away?"

"Because she doesn't want to marry Cassidy," Tom said. "She never would have agreed to if your father hadn't pressured her into it. Cassidy's one cold fish."

"He is not!" Carly shot up from her chair. "He's a very kind and—" A sudden burst of laughter from outside the office interrupted her. Relieved, she moved to open the door, gathering her thoughts as she went. The moment she looked out, she simply stared. Danny Gallagher was sitting at the edge of Susan Masterson's desk, fingering the thin gold necklace she was wearing. When they turned to look at her, Carly could only wonder at how much the laughter had changed Susan's appearance. She was actually pretty, Carly thought as the woman's smile faded and her expression turned prim again.

Clearing her throat, Susan said, "I apologize if I've disturbed you, Ms. Carpenter. Mr. Gallagher would like to join you and the others."

"I'm sure he would," Carly murmured, pushing the door wider so he could breeze past her into the room. When he had taken a seat, Carly closed the door and leaned against it. "Okay. What's up?"

"That's exactly what we want to know," Tom Chadwick said. "Ever since you came back into town on Sunday, this company has been in turmoil."

Danny laughed dryly. "The joke in the executive dining room is that the three-day storm that's been battering Manhattan can't compare to the one going on inside this building."

"Can you be more specific?" Carly asked.

"It's two days before her wedding, and no one, not even her secretary, has seen or talked to Jenna since Sunday," Mark said.

"Then there's the security people Cassidy hired when he came on board," Tom continued. "They've doubled in number during the last year, but for the past few days, either they're multiplying like rabbits or they're all on twenty-four-hour shifts. None of us are allowed into the family quarters upstairs. Even the executive chef is complaining. He has to send all the meals up on the dumbwaiter. This isn't Fort Knox, Carly. What the hell is going on?"

"His bride-to-be is sick. Perhaps Holt is overreacting a bit." Even as she said the words, Carly could hear how lame they sounded.

"And that's supposed to explain why your father summoned us, one by one, in to his office yesterday to give us the third degree?" Danny asked.

"We're not stupid," Mark said. "This security business began when we started working on the tea project. What's in those herbs you discovered? The cure for cancer?"

"No, of course not," Carly said, but a knock at the door interrupted her.

Susan poked her head in. "Do you want me to take notes, Ms. Carpenter?"

"No, that won't be necessary. Just see that we're not disturbed," Carly told her. Once the door was closed, she turned back to face the three men. Anger and hostility came at her in waves. But it wasn't directed at her. The men were angry at Holt. Moving quickly to Jenna's desk, she fished out a pad of paper and a pencil. "Okay," she said, glancing up at them. "I want to know all of the changes that have occurred here since Dad hired Holt, good and bad."

For more an hour, Carly took copious notes, and gradually a clearer picture began to emerge. The increase in security wasn't the main issue bothering the men. It was merely the tip of the iceberg, a symbol for the isolation they were beginning to feel because Holt's management style was so different from her father's. Finally, she laid down her pencil and faced the three men. "The bottom line is you don't feel that you're part of a family anymore. You feel like paid employees."

"*Mistrusted* paid employees," Tom added.

Rising, Carly picked up her notes and paced to the door, then turned back. There had to be something she could say, some way to make them see Holt's side of things. The problem was they didn't really know him. "Holt doesn't understand the idea of family," she said. "He's never had one." She glanced down at her notes. "You don't have any trouble with his ability to run the company."

"No." Mark glanced at his two companions. "I've been here the shortest length of time, but I'm impressed."

"No one questions his competence," Danny said. "He proved that when he took over while your father had surgery."

"And you're not jealous that Dad didn't choose one of you?" Carly asked.

"Perhaps at first," Tom said. "And maybe we would have been a little wary of anyone who tried to step into your father's shoes. But if we can reap the benefits without all the added pressure of actually running this company, why not? I just want to feel like I'm a part of the team again."

"I think you should talk to him, explain how you feel. Perhaps if you let him know that you trust him to run the company, he'll learn to trust you, too."

Carly searched their faces to see if she'd made any headway. But she couldn't read what they were thinking. "I know that my father trusts Holt, and I'd trust him with my life." It was just then that she realized they weren't even looking at her anymore but at the door beyond her. With a sinking sensation, she turned around to see that it was no longer closed. "Holt," she said. "I was just—"

"I heard." He glanced past her to the three men, who began to shift uncomfortably as soon as his gaze touched them. "Gentlemen, I'm sorry for the interruption, but the reporter from *Nation's Business* is here. Mark, I thought perhaps you and I could help Carly fill in for Jenna." With a short nod to the other two men, he took Carly's arm and led her out of the room. A short way down the hall, he handed her the paper cup he was holding. "Here, I thought you might need this."

The heavenly aroma of coffee filled the air. Before she could prevent it, the little tune she'd been humming to herself earlier slipped back into her head.

HOLT WATCHED the snowflakes whip against the window of Calvin's office. Behind him, he could hear the older man pacing. Time was running out, and Holt couldn't remember ever feeling so helpless. They'd been waiting almost an hour for the blackmailer to call. The phone would ring at any minute, and Calvin would have to make a decision. Unless they could think of something, anything that would give them an excuse to stall again.

Turning, he shifted his gaze to Carly. She was seated with her legs tucked under her on the couch, still poring over the file he'd compiled on Lance Bigelow, hoping to find something he and Calvin had overlooked.

From the time they'd arrived at the Carpenter Building this morning, the day had seemed to race by. There'd been no time to talk. He hadn't even had time to analyze what he'd been feeling.

There was desire. That hadn't stopped. He only had to look at her, at the way the light fell on her hair or the way a smile lit her face, and he wanted her. Making love with her had only made his need grow. And then when he'd heard her talking to Tom and Mark and Danny, when she'd said that she trusted him...

He hadn't believed her when she'd said she loved him. He'd been afraid to believe her, afraid to trust...

Calvin stopped his pacing right in front of Carly. "Well? Have you found anything, little girl?"

Carly raised her eyes from the file. "There's nothing here to suggest that Lance masterminded this affair with Jenna to get even with you for sending him away all those years ago. The brokerage firm hired him right after he earned his M.B.A. So he moved to Manhattan almost two years ago. In his business he would have known that Carpenter Enterprises had relocated here.

So he waits over a year to accidentally run into Jenna at Smiley's Health Club and Gym? Why wait so long if what he had in mind was revenge?"

"Humph," Calvin grunted, and clamped his teeth down on a cigar. "So that leaves us back at square one."

"There is one thing," she said. "Lance went to school in Atlanta. That's where Waterman Beverages has its main office."

Calvin whirled on her. "You think Sam Waterman has something to do with this?"

"Well, you did steal Mom out from under his nose. I was just thinking that if Sam knew Jenna and Lance's history, maybe he had something to do with getting Lance a job with Sterling Securities." Carly ran a hand through her hair. "I'm grasping at straws, I think."

"Sam came to your mother's funeral," Calvin said. "We buried the hatchet then."

Carly closed the file and rose to pace with her father. "Maybe we're looking at this from the wrong angle. Instead of worrying about who's out for revenge, we ought to try to figure out who the mole inside the company is."

"Mole?" Calvin asked with a frown.

"Traitor. Spy. Someone inside Carpenter Enterprises is involved, someone who knows about Carly's tea project and the research you're doing, someone who could plant a listening device in Jenna's bedroom. If we figure out who, maybe we can link that person with someone who wants revenge."

With a sigh, Calvin crossed behind his desk and sat down. "We're back to Mark and Tom and Danny again."

"No, I don't think so."

Calvin and Carly turned in unison to stare at Holt.

"That's a change of tune," Calvin said.

Holt glanced at Carly. "I think your daughter has a valid point. We've spent most of the day looking for something that would connect Lance Bigelow to someone in this company. I've assumed that he has the motive, and that someone at Carpenter Enterprises is spying for him. Maybe it's time we tried to figure out who the spy is and follow the trail to the person who wants revenge."

"So instead of narrowing the list of suspects, we should be adding names," Carly said. "It was a woman who was following Lance and Jenna to Bistro 720."

"But it was a man who followed us yesterday," Holt said.

"A small man wearing a ski cap," Carly pointed out. "And there was someone else driving the blue car. And it has to be someone who could get into our penthouse apartment and collect and replace the tapes in that recorder."

"This isn't getting us anywhere," Calvin grumbled as he picked up one of the computer disks and tapped it against his hand. "We're not going to have an answer in time."

As if on cue, the phone rang. Calvin punched the button on the speaker.

"Have you got the information ready to send?"

"I've got the disk right here in my hand," Calvin said. "Put my daughter on the phone."

"Tit for tat. The formula in exchange for your daughter's safety. Think of it as an insurance policy."

"Where's my daughter?" Calvin bellowed.

"Send the formula and the research to the address in your E-mail."

"Wait, I want to talk to her," Calvin insisted.

The only response was a dial tone.

"Damn," Calvin muttered. Then he looked at Holt. "We're not sure she's been kidnapped. She could be perfectly fine, enjoying her honeymoon."

Holt nodded. "But the blackmailer's message has changed. He's no longer promising she'll be back in time for the wedding. What he's offering is that she'll be safe. Perhaps that both your daughters will be safe. If you don't send the formula—"

The hum of the fax machine interrupted Holt. Grabbing the piece of paper, he laid it on Calvin's desk.

It was the headlines that jumped out at Carly as she joined the two men. Accident On The Slopes. Fatal Hit And Run. Pictures and a brief article followed each headline. Holt took the paper from Calvin's limp hand, while Carly watched the color drain completely from her father's face. Leaning down, she located the brandy and glasses in his bottom drawer and poured. As she pressed the drink into his hand, Holt said, "It's not about Jenna. It's just a threat calculated to scare you."

"It's succeeded," Calvin admitted as he set down the glass and drew in a deep breath. Carly slipped her hand into her father's. "I'll be all right, little girl." With his free hand, he picked up one of the disks and looked at it. "I don't want to send this to that bastard." Then he shifted his gaze to Holt. "You'll be running this company as of Friday. Perhaps this is your decision to make."

"We're damned if we do, damned if we don't," Holt said. "We can stonewall them and gamble that we can find Lance and Jenna before anyone gets hurt. But I don't think that they'll give up. If we send the formula and the research, we can guarantee both your daughters' safety starting right now." He turned to Carly. "I think this should be your call."

Carly simply stared at him as her heart turned over. In that one simple statement, he'd treated her for the first time as his partner. And there was even more. He'd given her his trust. Did he realize it? The little bud of hope that she'd been nurturing within herself all day began to bloom.

"Well, what is it, little girl?" Calvin asked. "Should I load this up and send it?"

Carly was about to nod her head when the door of the office flew open and Jenna burst into the room.

"Daddy!" Jenna raced across the room.

"My baby," Calvin murmured as he clasped her in his arms and held tight. Then he drew away to run his hands up her arms to frame her face. "You're all right?"

"I'm fine," she said.

Keeping his arm around her, Calvin shifted his gaze to the man who'd entered his office with Jenna. "You have some explaining to do."

"Yes, sir. I do," the man said.

"Daddy, don't start blaming Lance. I was the one who insisted we elope. He wanted to come to you from the start and explain how we felt. But I wouldn't let him. He finally wore me down last night and insisted we come back here and face the music. He said I wasn't being fair to Holt or you. Or Carly." Turning, Jenna took Carly's hand in hers. "I was especially unfair to you. I know that you never wanted to get married. It was selfish of me to have left you holding the bag." Leaning forward, she kissed Carly's cheek. "Lance and I have come back to try and make everything right."

Calvin gathered Jenna close again while he glared at Lance. "It was your idea to bring her home?"

"Yes, sir. I know that doesn't erase the fact that I agreed to the elopement."

"No," Calvin said. "But it does indicate that your judgment is improving. You know, if you'd tried something like this nine years ago, I'd have shot you."

Lance faced his father-in-law without flinching. "You might have had more reason then, sir."

Calvin's arm tightened on Jenna as he glanced down at the disks on his desk. With great satisfaction, he turned his computer off. "Well, your timing is improving, too. Tonight it was excellent. I owe you." Releasing Jenna, he moved toward Lance with his hand extended. "Welcome to the family."

Lance gripped the offered hand. "Thank you, sir. What can Jenna and I do to help with the damage control?"

Calvin's laugh bellowed out into the room. "Damage control? That ought to be a cinch after what's been going on here since the two of you disappeared. Tell you what." Clapping Lance on the back, he turned to Jenna. "On Friday you can walk down the aisle with my daughter and repeat your vows in a church, the proper way. We'll have a party afterward to celebrate your safe return."

"But what about the stockholders?" Jenna asked. "What about the fact that I'm not marrying Holt?"

Calvin looked at Holt. "I'm going to place that problem in Holt's very capable hands. He's very good at charming the stockholders. He'll have to be if he wants to run this company. In the meantime, sit down so we can fill you in on what's been going on while you were away."

"I STILL CAN'T BELIEVE it," Jenna said as she pulled champagne out of the refrigerator. "Someone used my elopement to blackmail Dad for the tea formula. Who would have thought?"

"Who would have thought I'd be in the kitchen helping you whip up something to eat while the men are planning to set a trap for the blackmailer," Carly muttered as she started to untwist the wire on the champagne bottle.

Jenna smiled at her sister. "It's called male bonding. You're the anthropologist. I'm sure you've run up against it in one of those cultures that fascinates you so."

"It's called **male** chauvinism, and it's kept women pregnant and in the kitchen for centuries. A situation I've never aspired to," Carly said as she sent a cork shooting to the ceiling.

"Then it's a good thing that Lance and I came back and rescued you from a fate worse than death." Jenna shoved the pizza into the oven. "Not that I thought we'd have much of a chance. I'm astonished that Dad didn't push for a double wedding on Friday. Or that Holt didn't insist on it."

Carly picked up a second bottle of champagne and aimed another cork at the ceiling, trying to ignore the pain in her chest. It had been growing ever since Holt had gone right along with her father's plan to charm the stockholders. Was that what a broken heart felt like? Kind of like heartburn, only worse. She'd have to record the sensations on a note card.

"I thought you said you'd ordered a salad, too?" Jenna said.

"I did. With sprouts." Carly pulled glasses out of the cupboard.

"Carly!"

Startled, she turned her attention to Jenna. Her sister had a bowl of salad in her hands. Behind her, there was a square-shaped hole in the wall.

"It's clear that you haven't been spending much time in *this* kitchen. You left food in the dumbwaiter."

Carly crossed to her sister's side. "Why would there be a salad in the dumbwaiter?"

"You ordered it from Mason, our executive chef, and he uses this to transport food from the kitchen downstairs."

Curious, Carly poked her head into the square hole. In the far corner she spotted a thin gold chain and picked it up. "It looks like he sent up his jewelry, too," she said. As she held it up to the light, a memory flickered and then faded. Turning to Jenna, she asked, "Does this look familiar to you?"

Jenna inspected it, then shook her head. "No, but Mason does favor gold, especially in earrings. He probably just dropped it while he was putting the salad in."

Setting the chain aside on the counter, Carly began to fill a row of glasses with champagne. The third time the liquid overflowed onto the counter, Jenna put a hand over her sister's. "What is it, Carly?"

Slamming the champagne bottle down, Carly began to pace. "I don't like being treated this way, sent off to the kitchen to do women's work. And besides, their plan might not work. Whoever is behind this would have to be *desperate* to walk right into Dad's office to look for the research disks."

"He was desperate enough to try to run you down on the street. I think Holt and Daddy are right. If I show up at my desk, fully recovered, at 9:00 a.m. and spread the word that Daddy and Holt will be out of the building all day, how will the blackmailer be able to resist looking for that disk?"

"We could be waiting all day for nothing," Carly muttered.

Leaning back against the counter, Jenna studied her sister. "This isn't just about the men plotting strategy in one room while the women cook in another, is it?"

"No...yes." Carly threw up her hands. "He's making me crazy."

"Holt?" Jenna's eyes widened. "You're in love with him, aren't you?"

"No...yes." To her complete horror, Carly realized that her eyes were filling with tears. Heartburn had never made her cry before. "I'm in love with him, but he doesn't want to marry me."

"That shouldn't be a problem," Jenna said, clasping her sister's hands in hers. "Lance didn't want to elope with me, either. I just kept after him until I changed his mind. Wait and see. You'll change Holt's mind, too."

Meeting her sister's eyes, Carly felt the terrible pain around her heart ease for the first time.

"Mmmrow," Priscilla complained as she walked haughtily across Carly's bedroom and jumped up on the bed.

"Kicked out, huh?" Carly asked. "Don't take it personally. They're newlyweds." She gave the hallway a quick search before she closed the door, but there was no sign of Holt. He'd still been talking with her father and Lance when she and Jenna had left the office. The men needed some time to discuss what they were going to say to the stockholders. And Jenna had wanted some time to prepare for her new husband. That had been almost an hour ago.

Closing the door, she faced Priscilla. "I, on the other hand, have been dumped. It's a little harder not to take that personally." She'd heard her father tell Holt to spend the night. Obviously, he'd decided to spend it in the guest room. Carly paced to the wall and whirled back to face the cat. "Jenna says if I just keep after him, I'll change his mind! Right! It's not that I haven't tried." She waved her hand at the boxes of notes stacked against the wall. "Been there. Done that. And now that Jenna's home, I'm stuck with the limitations of my own wardrobe." Passing the mirror, she wrinkled her nose at the plain white T-shirt she was wearing. Oversize, it hung off one shoulder and dropped in an unflattering line to midthigh. "Practical for nights on a tropical desert island, less than stunning for seducing a man."

Walking back to the bed, she plopped down beside Priscilla. "Besides, if I want to seduce him, I'll have to catch him first. Instead of taking so darned many notes on dating practices, I should have learned to hunt on that island. Or fish. Lu was a great fisherman."

"Mmmrow?" Priscilla said.

"Perked right up when I mentioned fish, didn't you?" Carly stroked her hand over the cat. "Lu's boat was always filled when he came home in the evening. I think that's what originally attracted Lania."

"Mmmrow."

"Not just because of the fish, silly. Lania was drawn by his competence. Lu was the most successful fisherman in the village. He spoke a little English, and when I asked him what his secret was, he laughed and said something like, 'Every day, I go out and fish.' So simple."

With a sudden frown, Carly turned her gaze to the door. "You know, maybe it is just that simple. Here I am waiting for Holt to come to me. But Lu never waited for the fish to jump into his boat." Rising, she began to pace again. "He's probably in the guest room right now, telling himself that I would be better off on Manilai. Or trying to convince himself that he'd be better off running Carpenter Enterprises by himself. He's used to people walking away from him. But he doesn't deserve to be alone anymore." Whirling, she walked toward the door. "And I'm not going to let that happen."

HOLT RACKED THE BALLS for the second time and wondered how long he'd be able to resist going to Carly. He'd convinced himself that she needed time. Everything had happened so quickly between them. They both needed a little time.

Taking careful aim, he sent the balls clattering across the table. Then, straightening, he tried to concentrate on the patterns the balls had formed. Playing pool usually helped him to relax. Or at least to focus his mind and think more clearly. But tonight he wasn't relaxed. And try as he might, he couldn't seem to get his mind off Carly.

As he circled the table, he thought back to Monday night when she'd been watching the game and taking notes. His lips curved at the memory, and he realized that he'd like to play with her. There wasn't a doubt in his mind that she'd be good. He'd seen firsthand how quickly she'd responded to that trainer's boxing instructions. And she'd make a challenging opponent because there'd be no telling which shot she'd take next.

With a sudden scowl, Holt walked to the corner of

the table. The game was supposed to take his mind *off* Carly. Leaning over, he took aim at the cue ball and hit it smartly. Two balls shot into pockets.

The whole evening was still spinning through his mind. The prodigal daughter had returned, and her family had welcomed her with open arms. Instead of recriminations and criticism, they'd offered Jenna unconditional forgiveness and love. Taking careful aim, Holt dropped a ball into the corner pocket.

All his life, he'd preferred to be the outsider, the onlooker. It was safer that way. And he'd never wanted a family. But in spite of that, he was being drawn into one. Lance had even asked him to be his best man during the ceremony on Friday. It would add a nice touch for the stockholders. But that wasn't the only reason that he'd agreed.

Frowning, Holt tapped the cue stick against the palm of his hand. When Calvin had offered him a position at Carpenter Enterprises, he'd accepted it for purely financial reasons. The only reason he'd agreed to marry Jenna was because it would give him the control he needed to run Carpenter Enterprises the way he wanted to. But something had changed.

He'd changed. And it had everything to do with Carly. From the moment he'd met her, she'd made him want more. Things that he'd never thought he would ever want again.

"Holt?"

Turning, he saw her in the doorway. He didn't speak. One look at her in that simple T-shirt had his heart thumping so loud he wasn't sure he could make himself heard.

"Waiting's hard," she said. She'd been watching him for some time, hoping for her system to calm. First there'd been the panic that had sprinted through her when she'd found the guest room empty, then the surge of relief when she'd heard the noise coming from her father's library. But those feelings had been minor compared to the ones that had been storming through her since she'd paused in the doorway.

It was exactly the same as when she'd first walked down the hallway of his apartment and seen him standing in front of the window. Except the urge to touch him was even more powerful. How could desire still be so sharp after all they'd shared, all they'd done in his apartment this morning?

The conservative shirt and slacks he was wearing shouldn't have been nearly as sexy as his running clothes. But then, it wasn't the clothes that drew her. It was the man beneath them. And when she took them off him, she knew what she would find. With her touch alone, she could make his skin heat and those smooth, beautiful muscles harden. She could make his heartbeat quicken and his breath shorten.

The realization made her confident enough to walk toward him. "When I'm waiting, I always like company." When she reached him, she could see his face more clearly. His eyes were unreadable and his expression implacable, and her courage almost faltered. Was she too late? Had he already made his decision? The fear made her bolder.

"We could play pool to pass the time," she said with a smile as she took the cue stick out of his hand. Turning to study the pattern of the balls, she lined up a shot. Thank heavens she'd taken those notes on Monday night. Quickly, she figured the angle, calculated the velocity and sent a ball careening off the side of the table. Two balls spun into pockets, the third rolled slowly, but inevitably, to its destination. Success bolstered her confidence.

Leaning the stick carefully against the table, she turned to Holt. "But I'd rather make love." Running one finger down his shirtfront, she paused to slip one button out of its hole. "And I know it's my call. I never got a chance to make it earlier because Jenna interrupted before I could tell Dad to send the research."

"Carly..."

Pressing her fingers against his lips, she raised her eyes to his. "No arguing. Those are the rules. You agreed, and now you're stuck." Removing her hand from his mouth, she ran her fingers lightly along his jaw, then down his neck to his chest.

"Carly, I..."

"Sh," Carly murmured. "No talking. You must be tired of doing that. You and Lance and Dad have been at it for hours. Plotting, negotiating. And all that time, I was thinking of doing this."

Starting at the top, she continued to unbutton his shirt. Each time she slipped her fingers beneath the material, she felt the tempting warmth of his skin. There would be heat soon. When she slipped the shirt off his shoulders and it slid to the floor, she felt a quick thrill. One look at his eyes told her he'd felt it, too. Her mind began to cloud. Fascinating.

Holding his gaze, she ran her hands down his chest, pausing to savor the pounding of his heart against her palm. There was such strength there, and kindness, too. If it was the power of the man that had drawn her at first, it was the goodness that had captured her heart. Moving her hand lower, she found the clasp of his slacks and drew down the zipper. A shudder moved through him. Delight mixed with her desire.

Bringing her hands back to his shoulders, she raised herself on her toes and drew him closer. "The first time you kissed me, I thought I knew exactly what it would be like. I'd been thinking about it a lot. But it was so much more than I'd expected. What will it be like this time, I wonder?" Briefly, she brushed her lips against his. Then, tempted, she pressed her mouth to his and took what she wanted. The heat, the excitement, the pleasure, everything she remembered streamed through her. But when he gripped her arms to pull her closer, she drew back. "It's still my call."

Slowly, she ran her hands down his arms, then up again. "Even before you kissed me, I wanted to touch you like this. That very first morning in your apartment, when I came out of the shower, I thought I would die if I couldn't do this." She brushed her fingers slowly over his collarbone, then down his chest. This time when she reached his slacks, she pushed them, along with his briefs, slowly down over his hips and legs, letting her fingers explore where they would. How could his skin be so smooth, the muscles so hard? So beautiful? She heard his sigh mix with a moan. So exciting. How incredible that she should have such power over him. The wonder of it filled her.

Holt shivered as she trailed her fingers up his calf. Her words, the gentle stroke of her hands had his head swimming and the breath backing up in his lungs. He'd felt desire before. In all of its facets, from a slow, sweet burn to a blazing fire. But this was different. Carly was different.

He could only groan when he felt the flick of her tongue at the back of her knee. He wanted to reach for her, but his arms wouldn't move. No woman had ever aroused him this way. No woman had ever made him ache with need. As her clever mouth made its way up his body, helplessness shuddered through his system. He was hers. The realization burned through his brain, destroying reason.

Grabbing her, he dragged her to the floor. He couldn't control his hands. They tore at her shirt, then ripped the thin swatch of silk that remained. He didn't even recognize his voice when he said, "I want you. Here. Now."

"Take me."

He thrust himself into her and let the madness take him as she completely enclosed him. When she arched against him again and again, matching his rhythm perfectly, he swore, not knowing he called her name. Faster and deeper he raced, determined to drive her, to drive himself higher until he no longer knew where he left off and she began. Until he no longer knew who was possessing whom. Until all he knew was Carly. Her scent, her taste, her body fused to his.

"Mine." He wasn't sure who said the word, only that it was spoken as they reached that final bright explosion of pleasure.

For a long time afterward, Carly felt as if she were floating through mists. Her mind was deliciously blank. Her body wonderfully limp and achy. And so alive, because Holt was with her. It was his ragged breathing she heard in her ear. His taste still lingered on her lips. And his damp, hot body still pressed to hers.

She couldn't move, didn't want to. But when she felt him start to shift, she found the strength to wrap her arms around him. "Don't move," she said.

"I was rough. I must have hurt you."

She opened her eyes then and saw the concern in his.

Slowly she smiled. "I'm not sure. I forgot to take notes."

She felt the laughter rumble up from his chest as he rolled so that his weight was off her. Then he framed her face with his hands. "It's not funny. I could have hurt you. You do something to me...I can't explain it."

Drawing him closer, she nipped at his lip. "Let me do it again."

"No you don't." With a laugh, he moved quickly to pin her hands above her head. "This time it's my call."

Carly grinned at him. "What do you have in mind?"

Very carefully, Holt touched his mouth to hers. Softly, slowly, he kissed her. She could feel her lips warm and soften and melt beneath his. One by one, she felt her muscles begin to liquefy. Then her thoughts started to stream away, too.

"I thought we'd try something different this time," he murmured as he nibbled along her jawline and gradually made his way to her temple. "Something with a little more elegance and restraint."

"Show me," Carly whispered.

And he did.

10

WHEN CARLY WOKE UP, the gray light of dawn was beginning to creep through her window. Shutting her eyes, she wished for darkness. If only the night could go on forever. The night and Holt. She was slipping lazily, softly into the dream when she felt the soft brush of fur against her cheek.

"Mmmrow."

Carly's eyes flew open, and she found herself staring into Priscilla's. Bolting upright, she realized she was sitting in her own bed. Alone, except for the cat.

The last thing she remembered was lying on the floor in her father's library with Holt. He must have brought her here, but he hadn't joined her. The hurt she felt surprised her, but she pushed it quickly away. Logically, she could understand it. There was a strong steak of integrity in him. Evidently it wouldn't allow him to sleep in her bed while they were unmarried and in her father's house. And that was as far as she was going to analyze his actions. Confidence was everything.

Throwing the covers off, she got out of bed and walked to the window. The snow had stopped, and the morning light was struggling through the clouds that still covered Manhattan. Far below, she could see the streetlights were still on, and here and there the headlights of cars pierced the darkness. Eventually, day would win the struggle with night.

And she was going to prevail with Holt.

A glance at her watch told her it was just after seven, so she knew exactly where he was. According to the plan, Holt and her father had to be out of the building by 6:30 a.m., leaving Calvin's office both tempting and accessible to the blackmailer.

Originally, Holt had wanted them all to leave. But she'd argued against it, pointing out how suspicious it would look if all of a sudden they all disappeared from the premises.

In the end, they'd struck a compromise. Lance would stay and guard the womenfolk along with two security guards. Jenna even got to play a starring role by arriving at her office shortly before nine and spreading the word that Holt and Calvin were out of the building for the day.

If everything had gone according to schedule, Holt and her father had left the building in a taxi about half an hour ago. By now they'd have had plenty of time to lose a tail and be seated in the coffee shop across the street, in a position to watch the two entrances to the building. They would be keeping in touch with the security guards by way of walkie-talkies.

In short, Holt and her father would be having all the fun while she and Jenna and Lance waited.

Crossing to her dresser, Carly pulled on jeans and a sweater. If she was going to wait all day, she might as well be comfortable. It wasn't as if she had nothing to do. She did have a book to write. She glanced at the boxes of notes stacked against the wall. Somehow, writing didn't have quite the same appeal now that she'd put some of her research to a more practical use.

And before she went back to more academic pursuits, she needed coffee. Grabbing the jar of instant out of her backpack, she headed out the door.

Priscilla was close on her heels as she walked down the hall. There was no sound from within when they passed Jenna's closed door, so she hurried on, stopping only when she saw the security guard sitting outside the door to her father's library.

"When did you come on duty?" she asked.

"At six-thirty when your father and Mr. Cassidy left," he said. "My partner's stationed inside the main entrance to the apartment."

Carly gave him a brief nod before she hurried on to the kitchen and closed the door behind her. "I hate waiting," she said to Priscilla as she turned a flame on under the teakettle. Then she found a bowl of cat food in the refrigerator. "I wish this whole thing was over."

"Mmmrow," Priscilla replied as she leapt onto the counter.

Carly was about to set Priscilla's dish in front of her when she saw it—the thin gold chain she'd found in the dumbwaiter the night before. Lifting it, she held it up to the light, and a memory slid into her mind.

Danny Gallagher sitting on the edge of Susan's desk and fingering her necklace. Susan's face transformed by laughter.

Her mind was racing as she continued to stare at the chain. It might not even be the same one. But if it was...

Setting the dish on the counter, she crossed to the dumbwaiter in three long strides and opened the door. If it *was* the necklace that Susan had been wearing, what was it doing in the dumbwaiter? Turning, she placed her hands flat on the edge of the shelf and levered herself up to sit on it. Then, ducking her head, she wiggled her hips and twisted so she inched herself backward. Finally, she drew her legs up until her knees were touching her chin.

"Mmmrow?"

Carly glanced over at the cat. "I'm just testing a theory," she muttered. She felt like a human pretzel, but she had managed to scrunch herself inside the small cubicle. The next trick would be to close the door. She reached for the handle. There was one inside as well as out, she noted as she tried it. She closed the door and quickly opened it again.

The next step in the test wouldn't be quite so easy. She hadn't liked the darkness or the sudden claustrophobic feeling she'd had in that brief instant when the door was shut. But there was only one way to complete the test.

Glancing down, she saw that Priscilla was now on the floor staring up at her. "Don't even think about it. I wouldn't be doing this myself if there was any other way. But if someone was using this to get in and out of our apartment, it would explain a lot." And it would also point the finger at the guilty parties, Carly thought. Susan and Danny. It was going to hit her father pretty hard, but it made a kind of sense. If Danny had been dating Jenna with the idea of one day becoming Calvin Carpenter's son-in-law, then he just might settle for a lucrative formula instead. It had been one of Holt's original theories. And who better than Susan to spy for him?

She should have seen it a long time ago. Susan was the closest person in the company to Jenna. Hadn't she and Holt discovered most of what they'd needed to know by studying Jenna's day planner? And who had easy access to it at any time?

The same person who had been in this dumbwaiter last night, sneaking into the apartment and listening at doors, picking up tapes from the voice-activated recorder. And there was only one way to test the theory.

"Wish me luck," she said to Priscilla as she pushed the down button, then snatched her hand back in and shut the door. Immediately, she heard the thrum of a motor and the dumbwaiter began its slow descent. To keep the panic at bay, she started to count. By five, she had a definite crick in her neck. By ten a cramp had started in her leg. Just as she was beginning to think that the dumbwaiter would never stop, it did. Twisting the handle, Carly shoved against the door and thrust herself out, feet first. She landed on a counter.

Drawing in deep breaths, she waited until her eyes adjusted to the dim light. She saw pots hanging overhead, a long counter down the center of the room. The kitchen. Sliding to the floor, she began to pace, reviewing what she already knew. A woman or a very small man could get in and out of her family's living quarters by using the dumbwaiter. A woman had been seen following Jenna and Lance. The "man" in the ski cap could have been a woman, too. And she'd found a gold chain in the dumbwaiter that had reminded her of the one Susan had been wearing.

It wasn't enough proof to take to Holt and her father. Turning, Carly made her way to the door and pushed through it to the executive dining room. As she wound her way past the tables, she glanced at her watch. Seven-thirty. Still early enough to check Susan's desk and perhaps even Danny's. On her way to the elevator, she spotted a light on in the lab. That meant Tom Chadwick had already arrived. She didn't have a minute to lose. The offices below could begin to fill any minute.

Hurry. The word formed a chant in her head as she stepped onto the elevator and punched the button. The moment the doors opened, she breathed a quick sigh of relief. The security lights were still on, and the place seemed deserted. Carly raced past the partitioned cubicles toward Jenna's office.

"YOU'RE SURE THIS THING works?" Calvin asked, frowning down at the walkie-talkie in his hand.

"It'll work as soon as one of the security guards has something to report," Holt assured him. "It's early yet."

And it was, Holt told himself as he glanced out the window of the coffee shop. So far the only person to arrive at the Carpenter Building was Tom Chadwick, and he regularly started work in his lab by 7:00 a.m. It was because of Tom that he and Calvin had decided to begin their stakeout early. The rest of the employees would begin to wander in between eight and nine. Then it would take time for Jenna to spread the word that he and Calvin would be out of the office all day.

Turning back to Calvin, he said, "It could be hours before anything happens."

"Humph," Calvin muttered as the waitress set mugs on the table. She filled Calvin's with the freshly brewed Carpenter tea he'd ordered, then she poured coffee into Holt's.

"I didn't know you drank that stuff," Calvin said.

"I rarely do," Holt replied. The truth was that he'd been as surprised as Calvin when he'd given the waitress his order. Was it his way of trying to keep Carly close? He'd been uneasy leaving her earlier, in spite of the fact that Lance was staying behind and two guards had been posted. It had been the one part of the plan that he'd liked the least. But Carly had been right. If they'd all suddenly cleared out of the building, it would have looked suspicious.

Worrying wasn't going to make the time pass more quickly. Taking a sip of his coffee, Holt said, "I have a feeling we're going to have a long wait."

Calvin glanced at his watch. "I hate waiting."

"So does Carly," Holt said.

Calvin met his eyes squarely. "Smart girl. You'll never find a better match." He raised his hands, palms out, in a gesture of surrender. "All right, all right. I won't say another word."

Holt's gaze held Calvin's as he leaned back in the booth. There was more than one way to pass the time. "No, let's talk about Carly," he said, and had the satisfaction of seeing surprise spring into the older man's eyes. "I have two questions."

"Shoot."

"First of all, I want to know if Lance was in on everything from the very beginning."

"In on what?" Calvin asked.

"On this elaborate plot you cooked up to marry off both your daughters and get yourself some grandchildren."

Calvin's eyebrows snapped together. "I don't know what—"

"You can bluff and bluster all you want, old man. But I know you, and I've got it pretty well figured out. I think it all started about six months ago when you had that open-heart surgery. You brushed up against your own mortality and decided you wanted grandchildren. Is that when you arranged for Jenna and Lance to meet?"

"I never saw or spoke to Lance until he walked into

my office last night with my daughter," Calvin protested.

"Maybe not, but it was six months ago that he and Jenna bumped into each other in the gym. Quite a coincidence, don't you think? I'm surprised it took me so long to figure out you were behind that little meeting. It wasn't until yesterday when you insisted on accompanying me to Sterling Securities so you could speak with Bill Cavenaugh personally that it suddenly dawned on me. If I had paid off someone nine years ago to stay away from my daughter, I would sure as hell have kept track of his whereabouts all these years. It took me a little longer to fathom why you didn't just invite the guy over for dinner."

When Calvin said nothing, merely sipped his tea, Holt leaned forward. He was beginning to enjoy himself. "Impatience isn't the only thing Carly inherited from you. She got her brains and her innate understanding of people from you, too. You know your daughters, probably better than they know themselves. Jenna's a romantic. So you concocted an Arthurian romance for her. An arranged marriage with me turns her into Guinevere running off with Lancelot, her true love."

"You're giving me far too much credit, boy," Calvin said.

"I'm not giving you *nearly* enough, you sly old dog. It must have given you a few bad moments when you had to worry whether or not Lance was behind the kidnapping. But maybe you knew him well enough to be sure he wasn't involved. And I have to admit, the really ingenious part of your plan was that the marriage you arranged between Jenna and me served a double purpose. Once Jenna jilted me and put the company stock in danger, you knew that Carly would come to the rescue. Because that's what Carly always does for her family."

Leaning back in the booth, Calvin studied Holt for a moment and then sighed. "It was a good plan. It almost worked."

"Was Lance in on it?" Holt asked.

"Good heavens, no. He's a romantic, too. An elopement was the best route for both of them. It was exactly what they were planning to do nine years ago."

"So Carly and I became the victims of their romantic fantasies?" Holt asked.

"I figured it couldn't do either one of you any harm. I never met two people more dead set against getting married and having a family. You were meant for each other."

"Then why didn't you word our agreement so that I would *have* to marry Carly when Jenna decided to elope?"

"Because in the end, no one can force anyone else to fall in love. Love can only be given freely. All I did was create opportunities. Lance didn't have to elope with Jenna. And you don't have to marry Carly. Unless you love her."

Suddenly the walkie-talkie blared to life with a blast of static. Calvin grabbed it. "Which one of these damn buttons do you punch?"

"Let me." Holt pressed the transmit button. "Cassidy here."

"This is Harrison in the penthouse. Miss Carpenter has disappeared."

"Carly's gone?" Holt asked.

"Yes, sir. She was in the kitchen feeding the cat. I heard the teakettle whistle. After a few minutes, I went to check on it, and she was gone. I swear she didn't get past me. But I've checked everywhere."

"Make sure that Mr. and Mrs. Bigelow stay put," Holt said as he slid out of the booth. "I'll be there shortly."

When Calvin started to rise, Holt said, "You stay here and follow our original plan. I'll take care of Carly."

SUSAN'S DESK WAS CLEARED, neat as a pin. Moving impatiently behind it, Carly began to open the drawers. She wasn't even sure what she was looking for when she spotted them in the bottom left drawer. Tapes. Small ones, small enough for a dictaphone or the voice-activated recorder she and Holt had discovered taped to Jenna's bed.

Quickly she slipped them into the pocket of her jeans. She needed something to play them back on. Glancing around, she was headed for Jenna's office when her gaze fell on the Rolodex. It was sitting on the small computer table behind Susan's desk, and it was opened to a name.

Waterman Beverages. Swiveling Susan's chair, she sat down to get a closer look. There were any number of legitimate reasons why the name of Sam Waterman's company might be in Susan's Rolodex. After all, Sam had been invited to Jenna's wedding. He'd also been an invited guest at a company party on Monday. There was even an E-mail address written in ink. And she bet it was going to match the one that was still in her father's E-mail in box. That would be proof enough.

"Thank you for joining us, my dear. We were hoping you would."

Carly's head jerked up at the sound of his voice. Sam

Waterman was walking out of Jenna's office. Susan Masterson followed close behind. As Susan moved forward, Carly saw the glint of a gun in her hand.

"This will make it so much easier," Sam said. "Now you can make up for all the trouble you've caused us by helping us get the information on those disks."

"It won't work," Carly said. "There are security guards in the penthouse, and the building is being watched. Someone saw you come in, and they'll alert the guards."

Reaching out, Sam gripped her chin. "Susan spent enough time in the penthouse last night to overhear most of your father's plan. So she and I never left the building, and no one knows we're here now. You've saved her a trip up in that dumbwaiter to get you."

"Sam, we need to get going," Susan said.

When Sam dropped his hand to her arm and jerked her up from the chair, Carly thought quickly. *Stall. Stall. Stall.* Any minute now the guard upstairs would notice she wasn't in the kitchen and notify Holt. She had to give them time to prepare. "You'll never get away. Someone will stop you when you leave the building, and they'll find the disks."

"We don't want the disks," Susan said, poking the gun into her back. "We're going to load it in the computer and send it. You're going to buy us the extra time we'll need."

They were halfway to the elevator when Carly stumbled. Sam turned to her, tightening his grip on her arm. "Please. I don't want to hurt you, Carly. I didn't want to hurt your sister, either. I loved your mother. She wouldn't want me to hurt you."

"If you loved her, why are you doing this?" Carly asked.

"Tit for tat. If your father hadn't forced her to marry him, you and Jenna could have been my daughters. Your father stole my future from me. Now I'm going to steal the future of Carpenter Enterprises from him. But I don't want to hurt you." When he raised a hand to run it down her cheek, Carly could barely prevent a shudder. His eyes were so calm. Too calm. And his voice. He could have been talking about the weather.

Leaning closer, he dropped his voice to a whisper. "But Susan's very annoyed with you. You nearly ruined our plan by proposing to Holt. And you've been so nosy. I just wanted to scare you. But Susan nearly ran you down with her car. She won't hesitate to use that gun."

Carly forced herself to take slow, even breaths as they half dragged her past the elevator and into the stairwell. "It was Susan who pushed me down these stairs, wasn't it?" she asked as they reached the first landing.

"I should have pushed harder," Susan said, jabbing the gun into her back. "Keep moving."

Carly tried desperately to think as they turned the corner and started up the last flight of stairs to the penthouse. But her mind was filled with questions. How much time had gone by? Would Holt be waiting? Impossible to know for sure. But one thing she was certain of. He wouldn't know that Susan had a gun. She had to give him some warning.

As Sam opened the door, Carly used all her strength to pull free, then turned so that her back was to the wall and Susan was at her side. "Sam, you've got to listen to me. You can't get away with this. Even if you succeed in sending the formula, my father will know you stole it. Susan's gun makes it armed robbery. He'll have you arrested."

Sam's voice was chillingly calm. "Your father will never prosecute me. He owes me. Tit for tat."

At the same instant that Sam stepped through the door, a fist connected with his face. Even as he fell like a rock, Carly flung herself at Susan, pushing all her weight against the arm that held the gun. The noise of the shot echoed in her head as they pitched together to the floor. The impact stole Carly's breath, and then she saw stars.

"CARLY!" Even as Holt screamed her name and lunged forward, the gun exploded for the second time. Holt saw the flare of the bullet just before the gun hit the floor and skidded across the carpet. Then he saw the bright red stain blossoming on Carly's sleeve.

Gripping Susan's shoulders, he hauled her off Carly and thrust her into the waiting arms of a security guard. Dropping to his knees, he ripped Carly's sleeve off at the seam. "You're hit."

"Yes," she said, staring at the blood as it flowed down her arm. "I can't feel it. Shouldn't it hurt?"

"Shut up! Just shut up!" Hands trembling, Holt examined the wound. "It's just a flesh wound. The bullet went right through. You're all right."

Saying the words out loud should have helped, but the fear rolling through him didn't subside. There was so much blood. He had to stop it. Glancing up, he yelled at one of the guards. "Call the infirmary. Get a doctor up here!" Pulling off his tie, he fashioned it into a tourniquet and applied the sleeve he'd ripped off her sweater as a pressure bandage for both entrance and exit wounds. Then he drew her into his arms and held her tight.

One of the guards had handcuffed Sam Waterman, another was doing the same to Susan Masterson. Even while he registered the details, Holt could still picture the bullet leaving the gun, the flash of fire and the bright red stain spreading on Carly's arm. Over and over, the images replayed in his mind. And each time, his heart stopped.

He might have lost Carly. He might have lost her! Fear and rage rolled through him.

Pushing her away, he tightened his grip on her good arm and barely kept himself from giving her a shake. "What in hell did you think you were doing?"

"I was finding proof."

"By trying to disarm a woman with a loaded gun? We had a plan. Why can't you ever do what you're supposed to do? What were you thinking?" His voice was rising. He couldn't seem to prevent it.

Carly lifted her chin. "*Thinking*? I was thinking she could shoot someone—"

"You." They shouted the word in unison.

"Time out! You two can fight about it later," Calvin bellowed as he stepped through the elevator doors. "The police are on their—" He stopped short when he saw Carly. "What happened, little girl?"

"I'm fine!"

"She's fine!"

Holt and Carly spoke the words in unison. And as Holt drew her to her feet and handed her over to her father, he finally began to believe it was true.

CARLY'S ARM WAS throbbing as she paced back and forth in her father's office. The initial numbness she'd experienced had worn off. The doctor in the emergency room who'd cleaned and stitched her wound and lectured her on how lucky she was that the bullet hadn't lodged in a bone had given her pain pills, but she hadn't taken them. She needed to talk to Holt.

But first she was going to have to find him. The moment she'd returned to the penthouse, Holt had disappeared. And gradually so had everyone else. First the police had finished up, then Calvin had gone to see Sam Waterman at the precinct where he was being held. Finally, Jenna and Lance had said something about running errands for a special celebration dinner.

Holt had said nothing at all. Not since their shouting match right after she'd been shot. He'd left without a word. It was her father who'd told her Holt had a meeting with the stockholders about the switch in grooms at tomorrow's wedding.

Holt was angry that she hadn't stuck to the letter of his plan. That much was clear. And perhaps he had good reason to be upset with her. Jumping a woman with a loaded gun hadn't been the smartest thing she'd ever done in her life. But all that had been on her mind was that one of the bullets might hit Holt. If she could ever find him, she might be able to make him understand.

But deep down in her heart, she knew that anger wasn't the only reason Holt was avoiding her.

And she didn't have a clue about what to do. It had been easier facing Susan's loaded gun than it was to face the fact that Holt Cassidy didn't want to marry her.

Why couldn't she just accept it and admit defeat?

"How about some brandy?" Calvin asked as he strode into his office.

"Why not?" Carly went to the bottom drawer of his desk and pulled out the bottle and glasses. It wasn't until he was seated in his chair and she handed him his drink that she noticed how tired he looked.

"How did it go with Sam?" she asked.

"I feel like an old fool. I thought that Sam and I had mended our fences at your mother's funeral. And all this time he's been blaming me." Calvin took a long swallow of his brandy. "The truth is, I did steal your mother from him. I can't get away from that fact."

Sitting on the edge of the desk, Carly covered his hand with hers. "Don't try to shoulder too much of the blame. Mom wouldn't have allowed herself to be stolen unless she wanted to be. And revenge wasn't the only thing motivating Sam Waterman, I'll bet."

"Smart girl," Calvin said. "I've known that Waterman Beverages has been steadily losing its market share over the past ten years. As people have become more health conscious, they're drinking fewer carbonated beverages. What I didn't realize was how that might affect a man like Sam. Evidently he's been treated several times for clinical depression. I think that he convinced himself that I not only stole your mother away from him, but I was also stealing away his customers. In that frame of mind, I might have been tempted, too, if someone like Susan had approached me and offered to pass along information. Once Sam learned about the tea formula and the fact that Jenna was secretly meeting Lance, he saw a way to get his revenge and build a new future for Waterman Beverages. No one was supposed to get hurt."

"Then why was Susan carrying a gun?" Carly asked.

"Good question. According to the police, they're both doing a lot of finger-pointing. My guess is that because Sam really loved your mother, he never intended to hurt you or Jenna and he was doing his best to restrain Susan." Lifting his glass, Calvin drained his brandy. "I hired Sam a lawyer. Would you think I'm crazy if I told you that I don't want him to do any jail time?"

Gingerly slipping her arms around him, Carly hugged her father. "I don't think you have anything to feel guilty about, but I think Mom would be pleased."

"It's not your mother I'm worried about. It's Holt," Calvin said. "I thought maybe you'd talk to him. Smooth it over."

Carly drew back and studied her father. "And just when would you like me to do this?"

Calvin glanced at his watch. "You could probably catch him now at his apartment. He headed there after we left the jail."

Carly took her father's chin in her hands so that he had to meet her eyes squarely. "You were behind all of this right from the beginning, weren't you?"

"I don't know what you're—"

"I should have figured it out when I was looking through Lance's personnel file. Bill Cavenaugh, the CEO at Sterling Securities, is an old friend of yours. I was so busy trying to find a connection between Lance and Sam Waterman that I missed it. *You're* the one who got Lance his job in New York. Then you arranged for him to run into Jenna, and you got her to agree to a marriage with Holt so she could jilt him. That way you could draw me into your little web of lies and deceit."

"Now, wait just a minute, little girl. Your mother wouldn't like to hear you talking to me that way."

"My mother would be cheering me on!" Carly said as she whirled on her heel and strode toward the door.

"Where are you going?" Calvin demanded.

"The one place I'm *not* going is Holt's apartment. Not until hell freezes over!"

IT WAS ALMOST COLD ENOUGH for hell to freeze over, Carly thought as she paid the taxi driver and stepped ankle-deep into a puddle of icy water. Hopping up on the curb, she tried to ignore the sound of her boots squishing. History was *not* about to repeat itself. This time when she proposed, Holt was going to say yes. Still, she couldn't quite rid herself of a feeling of déjà vu as she rounded the corner to the front door of Holt's apartment building.

But she had to see him, someplace away from her family. She had to talk to him. And one thing was different this time. She had no plan. Noteless and clueless, she had come to Holt's apartment totally unprepared.

At the last moment, she snatched her hand away from the doorknob. What was she thinking?

The *problem* was, she wasn't thinking at all.

Turning, she looked across Riverside Drive, trying to get a glimpse of the Hudson River. All she could see was a black void. Her future?

She shouldn't have come. The wisest strategy would be to wait, to give him time. But she *hated* waiting.

Turning, she opened the door and pressed the button. The moment the buzzer sounded, she pushed through the second door and strode toward the doors of the waiting elevator.

The door to Holt's apartment was open. Boots still squishing, she hurried down the narrow hallway before she could lose her nerve. He was standing at the window, just as he had been that first morning.

Need mixed with fear tore through her as she hur-

ried across the room. She had to tell him before she lost
her nerve. "I know you don't want to get married. I
know the last thing you want is a family. And I know I
should give you time. I *hate* waiting, but..." When he
would have spoken, she raised a hand to stop him.
Then she took a deep breath and willed her nerves to
settle. "Please, let me finish. You don't have to worry.
I'm not going to propose to you again. At least not yet.
Instead, I'm going to wait. I'll wait and wait until I
change your mind. And I won't ever stop waiting because I love you. And it has nothing to do with my father or Carpenter Enterprises. It has nothing to do with
my first proposal, either. I asked you then for all the
wrong..." Suddenly she stopped and fisted her hands
on her hips. His lips were twitching! "You're laughing
at me!"

"No," Holt said, even as the laughter escaped. But
when she whirled away, he was quick, taking her by
the shoulders carefully to keep her still. "I'm laughing
at us. Especially myself. You see, this time I can't wait.
So I made this plan. Jenna even went out to buy you a
wedding dress. But I should have known you'd spoil
it."

For the first time, Carly saw the candles. They filled
every surface, the desk, the mantel, even the hearth in
front of the fire. They shone as brightly as the stars lit-
tering the Manhattan sky. And then she noticed the
small linen-covered table that hadn't been there before.
Candlelight gleamed off silver and crystal. And an espresso machine.

Slowly she walked toward it. "You have an espresso
machine?"

Holt followed her to the table. "I bought it because I

know you prefer cappuccino to tea." When he turned her around to face him, he saw that her eyes were wet.

Suddenly, the nerves knotted tightly in his stomach. He reached out to touch the tear that was running down her cheek. "Am I ever going to know how to handle you? It wasn't part of my plan to make you cry. Come here." Uncertainly, he took her hand and led her to the fur rug in front of the fire. "Sit." Then he dropped to his knees in front of her. "Lord knows why I thought I could do this my way. It's probably a CEO thing."

"I'm sorry," Carly said. "Everything is so lovely. I wasn't expecting—"

"Shut up. I'm going to get through this. I even have a note card." He fished the card out of his pocket along with a small box. "I jotted down all the reasons why you should marry me. But we don't have to make it a double wedding on Friday. We can wait if you want."

Carly opened her mouth, but nothing came out. Her hands were shaking as she opened the box. The candle-light sparked off the diamond, making it shine more brightly than the stars. And then she saw the three words on the note card.

"Damn it, don't faint on me now," Holt said as he pressed a hand to the back of her neck.

But Carly wiggled away, then scrambled to her knees, threw her arms around his neck and began to rain kisses all over his face. "Say it. Say the words," she demanded.

His hands were trembling as he raised them to frame her face. He saw the laughter in her eyes and he saw the love. And he saw his future. "I love you, Carly." The joy that came from simply saying the words aloud poured through him, pushing the last of his fears aside.

"I love you. I wanted to spend my life alone. You've spoiled that plan, too. I can't live without you. Marry me?"

Her eyes were still bright with tears, but she was laughing as she pulled him back onto the fur rug with her. "I've got you, Holt Cassidy. And now that I do, you're stuck with me for a lifetime. Starting Friday."

"I can't wait," Holt said as he covered her mouth with his.

It's hot...
and it's out of control!

It's a two-alarm Blaze—
from one of Temptation's newest authors!

This spring, Temptation turns up the heat. Look for these bold, provocative, *ultra*-sexy books!

#679 *PRIVATE PLEASURES*
Janelle Denison
April 1998

Mariah Stevens wanted a husband. Grey Nichols wanted a lover. But Mariah was determined. For better or worse, there would be no more private pleasures for Grey without a public ceremony.

#682 *PRIVATE FANTASIES*
Janelle Denison
May 1998

For Jade Stevens, Kyle was the man of her dreams. He seemed to know her every desire—in bed and out. Little did she know that he'd come across her book of private fantasies—or that he intended to make every one come true!

BLAZE! Red-hot reads from Temptation!

Take 4 bestselling love stories FREE

Plus get a FREE surprise gift!

Special Limited-time Offer

Mail to Harlequin Reader Service®

> 3010 Walden Avenue
> P.O. Box 1867
> Buffalo, N.Y. 14240-1867

YES! Please send me 4 free Harlequin Temptation® novels and my free surprise gift. Then send me 4 brand-new novels every month, which I will receive before they appear in bookstores. Bill me at the low price of $3.12 each plus 25¢ delivery and applicable sales tax, if any.* That's the complete price and a savings of over 10% off the cover prices—quite a bargain! I understand that accepting the books and gift places me under no obligation ever to buy any books. I can always return a shipment and cancel at any time. Even if I never buy another book from Harlequin, the 4 free books and the surprise gift are mine to keep forever.

142 HEN CF2M

Name	(PLEASE PRINT)
Address	Apt. No.
City	State	Zip

This offer is limited to one order per household and not valid to present Harlequin Temptation® subscribers. *Terms and prices are subject to change without notice. Sales tax applicable in N.Y.

UTEMP-696   ©1990 Harlequin Enterprises Limited

THE MEN OF BACHELOR CREEK

Alaska. A place where men could be men—and women were scarce!

To Tanner, Joe and Hawk, Alaska was the final frontier.
They'd gone to the ends of the earth to flee the one
thing they all feared—MATRIMONY. Little did they
know that three intrepid heroines would brave the wilds
to "save" them from their lonely bachelor existences.

Enjoy

**#662 CAUGHT UNDER
THE MISTLETOE!**
December 1997

#670 DODGING CUPID'S ARROW!
February 1998

#678 STRUCK BY SPRING FEVER!
April 1998

by Kate Hoffmann

Available wherever Harlequin books are sold.

HARLEQUIN®
Temptation

It's a dating wasteland out there! So what's a girl to do when there's not a marriage-minded man in sight? Go hunting, of course.

Manhunting

Enjoy the hilarious antics of five intrepid heroines, determined to lead Mr. Right to the altar—whether he wants to go or not!

#669 *Manhunting in Memphis—*
Heather MacAllister (February 1998)

#673 *Manhunting in Manhattan—*
Carolyn Andrews (March 1998)

#677 *Manhunting in Montana—*
Vicki Lewis Thompson (April 1998)

#681 *Manhunting in Miami—*
Alyssa Dean (May 1998)

#685 *Manhunting in Mississippi—*
Stephanie Bond (June 1998)

She's got a plan—to find herself a man!

Available wherever Harlequin books are sold.